PENELOPE WARD
VI KEELAND

REBEL HEART

Editor & Formatter: Elaine York, Allusion Graphics, LLC
www.allusiongraphics.com
Cover model: Micah Truitt
Photographer: Leonardo Corredor
Cover designer: Sommer Stein, Perfect Pear Creative
www.perfectpearcreative.com
Proofreading: Eda Price

CHAPTER 1

Gia

I thought I might pass out. The room started to spin, and I had to grab onto Rush's arm to steady myself.

"Gia? You okay?"

When I opened my mouth to speak, a burn traveled up through my throat, a prelude to what I feared might be vomit following behind. I slapped my hand over my mouth, and somehow managed to mumble a coherent word. "Bathroom."

Rush guided me to a bathroom down a long hallway and tried to come in with me. He looked as nervous as I felt. I put my hand on his chest, stopping him from crowding into the little room with me. "I'm fine. Just give me a few minutes alone. It's just the morning sickness and my nerves."

"You sure?"

I nodded and forced a half-assed smile before locking myself into the bathroom. Sliding down the closed door, I sat on the floor with my head in my hands and started to hyperventilate.

It isn't possible.

My eyes are playing tricks on me.

Hormones. It's definitely the hormones.

I'd only seen Harlan that one night—months ago now.

But Rush's brother looked *so much* like him.

Those green eyes.

Perfectly tanned skin.

Square jaw.

Impeccably coiffed hair parted to the side.

But he wouldn't have been at The Heights.

Rush and his brother despise each other.

There is no way *that he came to hang out in the Hamptons.*

And...the guy I'd been with was named Harlan, not Elliott.

Although…

I'd always felt like it was a distinct possibility the guy had lied about his name. Something about the way he'd said *Harlan* struck me as off for some odd reason—like it hadn't rolled off his tongue as it should have. His speech pattern had been smooth, just like his lines, when he'd walked over and sat down beside me at the bar. But when he'd said his name, it came out with almost a bit of a stutter.

I suppose Elliott could have come out to the Hamptons to speak to his brother that night. Although there was definitely no sign of Rush when I'd met my one-night stand. And Rush is *not* the type of man I'd forget seeing.

The longer I sat on the floor, the more I made my head spin. I flipped back and forth from *of course it's him* to *it can't possibly be him* two dozen times in the span of five minutes.

A soft knock made me jump and hit my head back against the door.

"Gia. You okay, babe?"

The tenderness in Rush's voice made the tears start to flow. *God, what the fuck?* This couldn't be happening to me.

It was bad enough that I got myself pregnant with a one-night stand—it couldn't be *that* man.

Thirty seconds passed, and he knocked louder. "Gia?"

I had no doubt he would break down the door if I didn't answer immediately. "I'm good," I squeaked out. "Just a little nauseous. I'll be out in a few."

Over the next five minutes, I talked myself into believing that I had been wrong. Elliott wasn't Harlan. That would be ludicrous. I'd had a drink or two that night. It was someone who *looked* like him—from across the span of a wide room. Once I got up close, I'd realize he looked nothing like the man I'd slept with.

There were no other options to believe in here.

Eventually, after two more check-ins from Rush, a silent cry, and washing my face, I opened the door. Rush's hair told me he'd been yanking at the strands with worry. I reached out and patted the pieces down that stuck up.

"I'm okay. Sorry. That...just sort of came out of nowhere."

Rush breathed out a sigh of relief. "I'm going to be fucking useless in the delivery room. I can't even handle that you feel sick because I'm so worried that something is wrong."

My heart twisted in my chest. "You...you want to be in the delivery room with me?"

Rush's brows drew down. "Of course. I guess I just assumed I would be."

I looked back and forth between his eyes and felt myself getting choked up again. This time for a totally different reason. The man standing before me was truly amazing. He said the most beautiful things without even knowing it.

Rush didn't give his heart easily, but when he did—he gave a hundred and ten percent. He really was in this with me.

The pad of his thumb gently wiped away a tear that slipped down my cheek. "I don't have to be if you don't want me to be. Don't cry."

I threw my arms around his neck. "No. No. I want you there! I want you everywhere I am. I want you next to me through this entire thing. I just…I love you so much, and I guess I just realized for the first time that when you said you wanted to be with me…you really meant it. *With me, with me*…not just with me."

Rush's eyes crinkled, and the corners of his lips twitched. "*With you, with you.* Glad I cleared that up. I hadn't realized we weren't on the same page."

I kissed him. "Shut up. Just kiss me."

He licked my bottom lip. "I'm not gonna find any puke chunks in here, am I?"

I laughed. "You're so gross."

He licked my top lip. "What did you have for lunch…I am sort of hungry?"

For a few minutes, while the two of us hid in the corner outside of the bathroom, I completely forgot the panic of just a few minutes ago. Denial and self-protection tinted everything a rosy shade of pink.

"I heard a rumor that you were here." A man's booming voice popped the bubble of security I was enjoying so much.

Rush stiffened in my arms, and his grip on my hip tightened as he looked up and gave a curt nod. "Edward."

Rush's father had the exact same startlingly green eyes as his son and matched him in height and width, but the similarities ended there. Rush's eyes were filled with warmth while this man's were icy cold and distant. That might have been the reason goosebumps rose along my arms.

"Aren't you going to introduce me to your lady friend?" his father asked.

Rush spoke through gritted teeth. "Gia, this is Edward Vanderhaus. My sperm donor."

The man laughed. It was hearty and practiced. And also completely phony. It took less than thirty seconds to see firsthand why Rush didn't like him.

"It's lovely to meet you, Gia." Edward extended his hand to me.

I got the feeling that Rush might crack a tooth with how hard his jaw clenched when I hesitantly placed my hand in his father's. "Likewise."

Releasing me, Edward gripped one of Rush's shoulders. "Come join the party. There're a few investors here whom I'd like you to meet. Always good to show them that a family of shareholders has a united front."

Surprising me, Rush didn't make a scene. He nodded, laced his fingers with mine, and together we walked back out to the party with his father. Although some of my fingers might've turned white from the tight clasp he held my hand in.

I stood dutifully by his side while Edward introduced us to a few people, trying not to make it appear obvious that I was looking around for his brother. I needed a closer look, but he seemed to have disappeared.

Maybe the entire thing had been a figment of my imagination.

Hormones. *The hormones are screwing with me.*

I'd actually started to relax a bit again, lulling myself into believing that my mind had played a trick on me, when I suddenly caught sight of Harlan again across the room.

Or Elliott.

Jesus. He looked a lot like Harlan.

I couldn't stop staring.

I'd thought Rush had been engrossed in the conversation with his father and another man and hadn't noticed where my attention fixated, but I should've known he wouldn't miss a beat. He excused himself from the discussion and walked us over to one of the bistro-style tables that were set up around the massive apartment.

"Sir, would you care for a tartlet?" A gloved waiter presented a tray of what looked like mini pastries.

Rush lifted his chin. "What are they made of?"

"Caviar and crème fraiche"

Rush held up one hand. "Got any little hot dogs in the back? You know, for the non-asshole crowd?"

The waiter smirked and relaxed his rigid posture. "I'll see what I can rustle up."

I still couldn't take my eyes off Rush's brother across the room. God…maybe it wasn't him. From this angle, he looked different than I remembered. But his posture…his laugh…

"You know…" Rush leaned in and whispered. "…if you keep checking out my brother, I'm going to start to get jealous."

Shit.

I'd thought I was being discreet. Caught red-handed, I felt the need to make up an excuse. Of course, at the moment, a simple excuse such as *I was looking for a similarity between the brothers*, completely escaped me. Instead, I babbled.

"I can't help but think how much your brother reminds me of how I pictured a character in my book."

"Oh yeah? I hope you're talking about a villain, and not the hero who gets the girl in the end."

"Ummm…yeah. The character is sort of a jerk. He acts like a nice guy, but he's a phony."

Rush nodded. "Well, then you seem to have nailed that character in your book if he looks like my brother. Come on…let me show you the phony live and in person. We haven't said Happy Birthday to the guest of honor yet." Rush put his hand on my back and started to walk, but I stayed rooted firmly in place.

Panic set in.

"I don't think we should go over there."

Rush's brows furrowed. "Don't worry. He'll be polite to you. Big brother puts on a good show. He'll even act happy that I'm here…in front of people."

"It's not that…I just…"

"What?"

From the corner of my eye, I saw Rush's brother looking our way. He put a hand on the shoulder of the man he had been talking to and then shook hands as if he was wrapping up their conversation. When he took the first step toward us, I thought I really might be sick this time.

Elliott took a few more strides in our direction, and Rush caught him in his peripheral. "Looks like we don't have to decide to say hello. Your villain is heading right toward us."

I must've looked like a deer caught in headlights. Even though I had a naturally tan complexion and soaked up the sun this summer, I felt the color drain from my face. I had to be as white as a ghost.

"Well, isn't this a wonderful surprise," the blond Ken doll said as he approached with his hand extended toward Rush. "Lauren told me she invited you, but I figured you'd be too busy out east to stop by."

I couldn't help but stare. Did Harlan have so many teeth? Rush's brother's smile was so broad, it seemed like his mouth was crammed with pearly whites.

"Elliott," Rush nodded. "We were just going to come over and ask you how it felt to be an old man in your thirties."

Still frozen, I held my breath as the two men shook hands and then his brother turned his attention to me. The plastic smile on his face stayed firmly in place. "Elliott Vanderhaus…" He extended his hand and our eyes locked. "I don't think we've met."

Somehow I managed to raise my hand to meet his. Elliott's eyes were the same beautiful green color as Rush's, but lacked his brother's warmth and sparkle. Unlike Rush, whose eyes were a window to his soul, Elliott and Edward viewed the world through cold eyes that were shuttered and unreadable.

I wasn't sure if my hand was cold or his was particularly hot, but when he clasped his long fingers around my little hand, the heat made my palm start to sweat. When I didn't say anything for an unusually long period of time, Elliott prompted me. "And you are?"

I cleared my throat, and yet my voice still croaked. "Gia. Gia Mirabelli."

If my name rang a bell to him, Elliott hid it well. "Nice to meet you, Gia. My brother so rarely brings anyone from his personal life to meet his family. You must be someone very special to him."

Rush squeezed my hip. "She is. Which makes me realize maybe I was a little crazy for bringing her with me."

Elliott threw his head back with a deep chuckle. It must've been a Vanderhaus move that Rush luckily hadn't inherited. It struck me as an exaggerated response—one that was done more for show than an expression of true amusement.

"Well, it was lovely to meet you, Gia. And we're not half as bad as my brother will make us out to be. I promise."

He turned his attention to Rush. "Carl Hammond is here from England. He's on our board at Sterling Financial. I'd like to introduce you to him when you have a chance."

"Sure," Rush said.

Elliott reached out and squeezed Rush's shoulder offering a plastic smile. "I really am glad you came, little brother."

And just like that, Elliott turned and was gone. Seeing him up close, I would've sworn it was Harlan. But apparently I was wrong. He hadn't recognized me, nor did my name even ring a bell with him. Obviously, I was losing my mind.

I felt out of breath, and my heart pounded in my chest like I'd run a marathon, even though I hadn't moved. Just like what had happened that time I'd gotten in between two patrons fighting at The Heights, my adrenaline started to spike *after* the incident.

I had been wrong.

Harlan was not Elliott.

So why did I still feel so anxious?

"So...what did you think?" Rush grabbed two potato puffs from a passing waiter and handed me one. "Looks like every other annoying douche from The Heights who walks in with a whale or horse on his pastel polo, right?"

"Yeah. He definitely has a *familiar feel*." I wondered if someday I'd think what had just transpired in my head was funny and tell Rush all about it. Somehow I doubted it.

My brain was still a jumbled mess from the scare of my life, and I needed another minute to myself in order to get my emotions back in order. Not to mention, the extra water that I'd been trying to drink every day had my bladder feeling full. "I'm sorry. I need to use the ladies' room again."

Rush pulled me close. "Want me to come with you? I'd give my left nut to make your moan sing out over the expensive audio system they have blowing elevator music through this place."

I smiled. "I don't think that's a great idea."

Rush walked me back to the bathroom. "You have your phone, right?"

"Yes, why?"

"Pick it up when I call you. Just listen. I'll give you some new material for your phony book character."

I squinted. "What are you talking about?"

He kissed my forehead. "You'll see."

Inside the bathroom, I actually did need to go this time. I relieved myself and started to wash my hands, when my cell rang from my purse. I dug it out, and automatically said hello, even though Rush had told me just to listen.

"Which one is Carl Hammond? The guy you wanted me to meet?" Rush's voice was a bit distant. He wasn't talking into the phone, just holding it to pick up the interaction with his brother. I turned up the volume to eavesdrop, which is apparently what he wanted me to do.

"Pretend you have some class when I introduce you. Maybe start a conversation about the weather or the stock market rather than tattoos and trailer parks." The tone of the voice was filled with disdain, but there was no mistaking it belonged to Elliott. A *very different* Elliott than I'd just been introduced to.

"Since Hammond's British," Rush said. "I figured I'd ask him if he knew Maribel Stewart. You know, the woman whose throat you had your tongue down last month at the board meeting. I saw you in the hall with her before the vote."

"My tongue isn't the only thing that Maribel likes to have down her throat."

"You're a pig. I have no idea how you look your wife in the eyes."

"Speaking of women…" Elliott trailed off. "*Gia* looks familiar. Have I met her before?"

My eyes widened.

"No. And don't plan on meeting her a second time. She's too good for you, and I never should have brought her here in the first place."

The sound of a third man's voice interrupted the heated conversation between Rush and Elliott—a man with a British accent. I listened for a minute more while Elliott seamlessly changed back to the gracious host and introduced Rush to the man. My head started to spin again.

Could Elliott be Harlan?

Did he pretend to not know me?

He'd said I looked familiar. From the conversation they'd just had, clearly, Elliott cheated on his wife.

Fuck.

I was making myself crazy.

If he were Harlan, he wouldn't have pretended to not know who I was.

The Elliott who just spoke would *love* to tell his brother he'd slept with his girlfriend.

Wouldn't he?

With the animosity between the brothers, I was positive that Elliott would get off on telling him that he'd had me.

But then…

Rush would make a scene.

Elliott's wife would come running.

And then what?

How would he explain to Lauren why he'd just been punched in the face?

A knock at the bathroom door startled me out of my thoughts. "One minute."

I just needed to get out of here. Get Rush and get the hell out of this place. Go back to our little bubble in the Hamptons and forget tonight ever happened. No good could come from being here and debating this in my head. And stress was not good for my baby. *Elliott's baby?* God, it couldn't be.

So, straightening my makeshift dress, I took a look in the mirror, patted down my unruly curls, and closed my eyes for a few cleansing breaths.

I opened the door just as the second knock came and was greeted by a face that I didn't expect on the other side.

Elliott.

Or Harlan.

"Gia." His face slid back into that perfect, toothy smile. "I didn't realize it was you in there."

I looked both ways down the quiet hall. "Where's Rush?"

"I left him to talk to a board member. Is everything alright? You look a little pale."

"Umm. Yeah. I just…I don't feel so great. I think it might be something I ate." I pointed toward the party needing to get the hell out of there. "I'm going to go grab Rush and see if he can take me home."

Elliott searched my face. "You look very familiar. Have we met before?"

"No," I snapped.

His brows drew together.

The urge to flee was strong. I needed to get ahold of myself—calm down. "It was nice meeting you."

Elliott stood in place, watching me. "Yes. You, too."

I stepped from the bathroom doorway and took a few long strides down the hall. Getting to the end, I spotted Rush engrossed in a conversation with an older gentleman on the other side of the apartment. No one was in the vicinity at all.

And…

I needed to know.

Who was I kidding?

If I left without knowing for sure, I'd never be able to relax. It would eat at me for days. Months. *Years.*

With another burst of adrenaline spiking, I turned around and took a deep breath. Elliott was still standing there watching me when I marched back to stand in front of him.

"Actually…you look familiar to me, too."

The wheels in Elliott's head were turning as he continued to try to figure out where he knew me from.

God, this was nuts.

But I needed to know.

I looked him straight in the eyes. "You look like someone I met once in the Hamptons. At The Heights, actually. Maybe you know him?" I took one last deep breath and spit out the rest. "His name is Harlan."

Elliott's narrowed eyes grew to the size of saucers as a look of recognition finally hit. Then the sleaziest smile spread across his face.

"*Gia*—you came back for seconds?"

CHAPTER 2
Rush

"You sure everything is okay?" Gia had seemed a little off ever since the party last night. She was quiet on the drive home, and when I initiated fooling around—something that she never refuted and often initiated herself lately—she'd said she had a headache and was tired. Now she was staring down at her bowl of cereal like she needed it to give her the answers to all of life's questions.

She blinked a few times and looked up at me, but her mind was clearly still somewhere else. "I'm sorry. Did you say something?"

"I asked if you would mind if I had my cereal with your breast milk once it starts to come in."

She absentmindedly reached for the container of milk sitting next to her bowl and handed it to me. "Umm. Sure. Here you go."

At best, she heard fifty percent of what I'd said.

My chair scraped along the tiled kitchen floor as I pushed back from the table. I pulled Gia's seat back, scooped her up, and sat my ass down with her on my lap. Slipping two fingers under her chin, I made sure I had her attention this time.

"What's going on? Something's bothering you. You've been acting strange since the party last night. Did getting to see Satan and his spawn freak you out about being with me?"

"What? No!"

I pushed a lock of hair behind her ear. "Then what's bothering you? Talk to me."

"I…" She shook her head and looked away. "I don't know. I'm just really tired all of a sudden, and…even though I've made progress on my book, the deadline is really starting to weigh on my mind."

I nodded. "I bet my brother reminding you of the villain in your book brought that all to the forefront of your mind. The douche's face can ruin anyone's day."

She nodded. "Yeah. That's probably it."

I kissed her forehead. "I'll tell you what. I have business to take care of today, anyway. Why don't I motivate you to write all day? What's a good day of writing for you?"

She shrugged. "Maybe three thousand words."

I smirked. "Pretty sure that's more than I wrote in four years of high school and one of college before I dropped out."

"You went to college?"

"Yep. School of Visual Arts. I wanted to learn animation. I had this crazy idea of animating an adult cartoon series based on my winged babes. Not cartoon porn…but sexy babes who can fly and fight crime."

"That's not crazy. I bet it would be amazing if it turned out anything like your art. But why did you drop out after a year?"

"My mother told me that my father had set up a college fund and was paying for college. During my second semester, I was looking through her file cabinet for a copy of my birth certificate to apply for a passport, and I found a bunch of loan documents. My father hadn't paid for college. She was pulling equity out of her house to pay the tuition each semester. By the time I hit third year, she would've been mortgaged for more than her house was worth." I shrugged. "I told her college wasn't for me and dropped out. There was no way that I was letting her take on all that debt when she'd worked her ass off to pay down that mortgage for twenty years. My plan had been to work a year or two, save some money, and go back when I could afford to pay the tuition myself."

"But you never went back?"

"Nope. I found tattooing and then eventually I came into the money that my grandfather had left me, and my life took a different direction after that."

"Does your mom know the real reason you dropped out?"

"No." I pointed a finger at her. "And if she finds out now, I'll know where the leak came from. You're the only one I've ever told that story to."

Gia let out a big sigh and clasped her hands behind my neck. "You're a good man, Heathcliff Rushmore. Such a good man."

My brows lifted. "Heathcliff, huh? You better watch it. I was thinking your reward for pounding out three thousand words would be I'd pick up a chick flick DVD, a big ass container of Chunky Monkey with two spoons, and bring some massage oil so I can rub the tension from your neck after typing all day. But…if you start calling me Heathcliff, I'll be bringing girl-on-girl porn, eating an ice cream cone for one on my way over, and you'll be using that massage oil to slick my wick while I sit back with my hands behind my neck and you do all the work."

Gia graced me with the first genuine smile since last night, and I felt like I'd seen the sun after a month of gray skies. It made me realize how deep I really was in with this girl. There wasn't much I wouldn't do to make her happy.

I kissed her lips. "I'm gonna head out to let you do your thing. How about if we stay at my house tonight so we have privacy? I'll pick you up after you finish writing."

"Okay. That sounds good."

I reluctantly lifted Gia off my lap and set her back down before going to grab my car keys and wallet from where I'd left them in the bedroom.

"Type your heart out," I said before kissing her goodbye on the lips one last time. "Because we don't like it when you're stressed." I bent and kissed her belly. "Right, little guy? We like Mommy calm and smiling."

———

That afternoon, I still had a few hours to kill before it was time to pick Gia up. I found myself wandering around the center of town, wanting to buy her a gift that might cheer her up. The problem was I just didn't know what to get her.

The craving for a cigarette was enormous. I sucked on a toothpick to try to curb my urges, but it wasn't helping. Tossing the toothpick in a trash bin, I cursed under my breath, so disappointed in my weakness.

My two vices were smoking and sex, and I was finding out how difficult it was to give up one without the other. I had neither smoked nor fucked in the past twenty-four hours, and it was really screwing with me. I walked around feeling completely unbalanced, on the verge of getting the shakes.

But I needed to focus my attention off of my little problem and onto Gia. Her mood from last night and this morning was definitely peculiar. I would've done just about anything to make her feel better.

Walking by a local thrift shop, I happened to notice something in the window that stopped me in my tracks.

Wow.

Bingo.

I might have just found exactly what I needed. This was it; she was gonna love it.

A bell on the door rang as I entered the store that smelled musty, like old clothes and shoes. A feeling of nostalgia hit me, because being in here reminded me of trips to the Salvation Army store with my mother growing up. We used to buy a lot of my clothes there. I remember getting all excited to go. At the time, all the stuff was new to me, so in my eyes there was no difference between going there or to a department store. Mom would always let me pick out a toy. It was just "the store" to me. And they always carried stuff you couldn't find anywhere else, things that weren't even made anymore. So in some ways it was even cooler than a real store. I never questioned why the bags they gave us to hold our stuff had no name on them. And you know what? Getting my Salvation Army toy, in retrospect, had been more exciting than having the means to buy anything I wanted now, because I had appreciated it so much more.

I put down a set of old trading cards I'd been holding when the attendant entered the room. Fuck, she smelled like cigarettes, and my craving came back in full force.

"Excuse me?" I said to her. "How much is that doll in the window?"

"Are you kidding? I'll *pay* you to take it away. That thing scares the living daylights out of me. It's why I have it facing out toward the street and away from me. It's more like a Halloween decoration at this point."

I chuckled. "I'd like to give it a good home. I know someone who will really appreciate it. But I don't feel right not paying for it. Can I give you something?"

"A dollar is fine."

I took a ten out of my wallet. "Here. Ten?"

"Thank you. That's more than generous for that thing."

She went over to fetch it from the window then blew some dust off of it. The particles hit me in the face as she handed the doll to me.

When it came to Gia's collection, the uglier the better. The funny thing was, my mother had purchased another kind of doll for her, but I hadn't given it to Gia yet. There was no doubt she was going to like this one more. It had long, black hair that was knotted and messy, almost like it had been electrocuted. Its head was huge compared to the body, and the eyes were unusually big like saucers with eyelids that opened and closed when you moved her head. The only thing she was wearing was a stained white shirt with no pants. It almost looked like a straitjacket. *Where are your pants?* This thing was a gem.

"Thanks again."

"No, sir. Thank *you,*" she said.

I shook my head in laughter as I made my way out of the store with the doll in hand.

I walked about a block, and headed toward my car before spotting what looked like Oak's Cadillac drive by. It stopped before suddenly reversing.

"Hey, Rush!" Oak rolled down the window and nudged his head toward the doll. "Something you want to tell me, man?"

I couldn't help but laugh. "It's for Gia."

"You mad at her or something?"

Looking down at it, I said, "Nah. She actually collects ugly dolls. It's a hobby."

"Well, then I'd say you got it right. Because that is one ugly ass doll."

"Yeah. That's why it's perfect."

He stuck his head farther out the window. "You need a ride or something? Why are you walking?"

"No. My car is parked a few blocks away. I just decided to walk around town, blow off some steam."

Oak pulled over to a parking spot before getting out and joining me on the sidewalk. He looked me up and down with a big, goofy smile on his face.

His stare prompted me to ask, "What?"

"Never thought I'd see the day my man Rush was buying dolls for his sweetheart. Life is damn funny."

"Hysterical." I rolled my eyes. "Well, glad I could amuse you. Gia's been feeling kind of shitty. So hopefully this will cheer her up."

"Pregnancy hormones?"

"I think so. She's just been down. I dragged her to a party at Elliott's, and I almost wonder if it was too much for her under the circumstances. She's been in a funk ever since. You know…like she thinks she looks fat when she's never been sexier."

"I hear you. Well, I guess it's normal to feel out of sorts in her condition."

"Yeah. I've heard pregnant women just get that way from time to time."

Oak placed his hand at his forehead to block the sun from his eyes. "How are you holding up?"

"What do you mean?"

"I mean…this is a big adjustment for you, Rush. It's not just Gia whose life is changing forever. Has anyone asked how *you're* doing?"

That was an interesting question. I was too wrapped up in Gia to dissect my own feelings. But I knew a few things to be true.

"Honestly? I've never been happier. I've also never been more scared about anything. But I'm taking it one day at a time. Moment by moment. And right now? I just really need a fucking cigarette."

"I noticed you haven't been smoking lately. Good for you."

"Good for me if I don't kill anyone in the meantime, yeah. It's harder than I thought."

"Resist that shit, Rush. The sooner you quit, the better. Been twenty years for me." He put his hand on my shoulder. "You're gonna be just fine. If you ever need to vent, you know you can talk to me, right?"

"Yeah." I nodded.

Oak was a good friend. I messed with him all the time, but the truth was, I'd never do anything to hurt him, would never fire him in a million years. He was one of the few people I trusted. Not to mention his big, burly ass could flatten me if I ever crossed him.

"Alright." He opened his car door and got back in. "I'll see you tomorrow night."

I called out, "Hey…uh, can we not repeat this to anyone at The Heights, that you caught me carrying a doll?"

Oak leaned his head back in laughter. "Don't worry, boss. Your secret's safe with me. Although, might be fun to hold this over your head the next time you threaten to can me."

———

I made sure everything was set up for Gia at my place when we arrived that night. The Chunky Monkey ice cream was in the freezer, and I'd picked up a pre-made lasagna at the Italian restaurant in town that I planned to pop into the oven for dinner.

She spotted the doll right away as she walked over to the center of my kitchen table where I'd propped it up against a vase of red roses.

Her mouth curled into a rare smile. "What did you do?"

"Surprise."

Gia lifted the doll and took her in. "She's…oh my God… she's…"

"Ugly as fuck." I crossed my arms, smiling proudly.

"I was gonna say…perfect. But *so ugly*, yes. Which makes her perfect. Where did you find her?"

"I got lucky. She was sitting in the window of the local thrift store just waiting for me, waiting for us to find her, to give her a good home."

She clutched the doll to her chest, but her reaction was unexpected. She started to cry.

Fuck.

This was supposed to cheer her up, get her out of whatever funk she was in, not make her sadder.

"What's wrong, Gia? This was supposed to make you happy."

She looked up at me before wiping her eyes. "Nothing. Everything is perfect."

Gia put the doll down and wrapped her arms around my neck. She still had tears in her eyes when she leaned in. Her kiss was hard and intense as she raked her fingers through my hair.

"Take me to your room," she said.

"Now? We haven't eaten yet."

Then it hit me. What was I smoking? Crack? Had I become hormonal like Gia with the pregnancy? Why was I questioning it? *Hello?* She wanted to have sex. Giddy up!

She spoke over my lips. "Yes. Now."

"You don't have to ask me twice."

When it came to wanting sex, she'd gone from cold last night to completely hot today. Fuck if I was gonna complain about that. I was either going to fuck her tonight or fall off the wagon smoking an entire carton, so I was happy she was in the mood.

I carried her upstairs to my bed. As I hovered over her, she spread her legs wide open.

"Look at you…all ready," I teased.

Gia was super wet lately. She always said being pregnant made her arousal ten times stronger, and she wasn't kidding. She was so incredibly lubricated when I sank into her, and it felt damn phenomenal. It had only been a little more than a day, but it had seemed like forever since I'd felt this.

She pulled me so tight against her as I fucked her good and hard. I couldn't help but feel like she was holding onto me for dear life.

CHAPTER 3

Gia

I hadn't told a single soul. And it was eating away at me.

As Rush slept, I just kept staring at his handsome face wondering how many more mornings I would have like this, where I would wake up feeling protected and loved, where Rush wouldn't be broken and devastated.

Last night had been so amazing, but it was tainted by the enormous guilt I felt. After we made love, Rush served me the most delicious lasagna. Then we watched a movie while eating ice cream out of the container. He gave me a foot massage until I fell asleep on the couch. He must have carried me to bed because I don't even remember how I got here.

Now it was morning, and the sun was pouring in through the French doors that led out to the balcony. The waves of the nearby ocean were crashing amidst the sound of the seagulls' morning call. Waking up at Rush's place was heaven. I cherished each and every second of this peace. But it was bittersweet, knowing that the calm would likely be short-lived.

I went back and forth on how to handle things. Some moments, I was pondering never telling him the truth. Others,

I couldn't fathom keeping this secret. For a millisecond, I'd even considered running away and never coming back because I couldn't deal with the shame.

A part of me did wonder whether I could get away with never saying anything, that maybe Elliott would never question the baby, and that everyone would just assume it was Rush's child.

The other part of me, the much bigger part, knew that I couldn't live with this secret for the rest of my life. It would kill me. Every time I would look into Rush's trusting eyes, a piece of me would slowly die from the guilt. Protecting Rush was my number-one priority. Not to mention, if Elliott ever said anything about his tryst with me, Rush would put two and two together. Elliott could very well hold this over me until just the right moment to unleash it. He couldn't ever be trusted.

There was no way out. I had to tell Rush that his brother was the father of my baby. I cringed at the thought, unable to even think those words. It was just unfathomable. It didn't matter how many times I'd said it to myself, it just didn't seem real.

I felt like I needed to confide in someone first, but there were very few people I trusted—basically Rush and my father. Riley was a good friend, but I couldn't risk even the small chance that she would tell someone. Confessing the pregnancy to her had been one thing. But this? No.

It was becoming clearer and clearer to me: I had to tell my father everything.

Rush's body stirred, snapping me out of my thoughts. He rolled over and pulled me in for a kiss. He was gloriously hard as he often was when he woke up.

"You slept well," I said.

His voice was groggy. "You didn't?"

"Not really. I've had a lot on my mind and terrible heartburn kept me up."

More like heartbreak.

He suddenly got up from the bed.

"Where are you going?" I asked.

"I'm going to get something. Be right back."

When he returned to the room, he was carrying another doll, but this one looked exactly like a real baby. And it wasn't ugly at all.

"What is that?"

He looked down at it and chuckled. "So my mother had this idea. I told her it was stupid, but she insisted. This thing is supposed to simulate a real baby. It can be programmed to cry at certain times and a bunch of other things. She said she wished she had one of these when she was pregnant with me."

He placed it in my arms. It felt how I imagined a real baby to feel. It was a boy, dressed in a light blue, footed sleeper.

He continued, "So we can set it to go off at certain times. That way we can get used to getting up and shit, so it's not such a shock when it really happens."

I looked down at its realistic face with creamy skin and perfect bow lips. "Wow. I didn't even know this kind of thing existed. It feels and looks just like a real baby."

"And it's not even on. The limbs move, too." He took it from me and pressed a button that was located at the back of the doll. It started moving its arms and legs and even made cooing sounds.

"That's freaky, Rush. You look like you're holding an actual baby."

"Except *our* baby will be a fuck of a lot cuter." He winked.

Our baby.

His words were like a punch to the gut.

"It burps and a bunch of other stuff," he said, continuing to hold it as he stood across from the bed. "Anyway...I thought maybe it was too soon. But when you said you'd been up thinking, I thought maybe the sooner we could get used to the idea, the better."

He was rocking it gently, and I didn't even know if he realized how naturally that seemed to be coming to him. The sight of this strong, tattooed god of a man rocking this baby doll was just about the best and most bittersweet thing I'd ever witnessed.

Oh, Rush. You're killing me here.

My heart was breaking because a part of me knew that this might be the only way I could ever experience this with him.

———

The next day, I sat in my father's living room in Queens and watched the man who was my hero, my strength, break down in front of me.

All of the lights were off. We hadn't even noticed when daylight ended and never bothered to turn them on. I'd never seen my father cry—until now. And to think that I had caused it. This was just a prelude to the feelings of pain I would be experiencing soon.

For the past hour, I'd not only told him I was pregnant but ended up confessing the unthinkable situation I'd gotten myself into with Rush's brother.

"Say something," I said to him. My father was just sitting there in his NYPD uniform for the longest time with his head between his hands.

He finally spoke. "I just feel so badly for you, honey. I don't know what to say that's going to make you feel better. You're just going to have to go through all of this. And you have to face Rush."

"You're not mad at me? Because I feel like I've completely disappointed you."

"Mad? No. A little *sad*, maybe. I know this is going to make your life a lot more difficult. And I honestly wish I had a solution on how to handle Rush, but I just don't. You have to tell him. And you need to do it soon."

The thought of that filled me with dread as I whispered, "I know." I lay my head down on a pillow. "I don't know how I'm gonna deal with everything when Rush is gone. He's been such a source of strength for me."

My father got up and poured us each a glass of water.

He sat back down next to me and said, "Let me tell you a story about your mother that you don't know."

I sat up and gulped down some of the water. "Alright…"

"Even from the beginning, when she was pregnant with you, I always had a strange inkling that she might not stick around. Don't ask me how I knew…it was intuition, maybe. She just wasn't cut out for parenting. And you know…I was scared shitless when I found out about you, too, in the beginning. Terrified, even. But, baby girl, when you came out and I took one look at your face…all of that fear, it transformed into something different. The fear was no longer about whether or not I could love you. It was about protecting you, keeping you safe because I loved you so very much. I still do."

"Thank you, Dad."

"But here's the thing…I quickly learned that there wasn't anything I wouldn't do for you and that I really didn't *need* anyone else. The strength was within me all along. You brought it out in me. And I know that no matter how hard this seems, you have the same strength in you. You don't need Rush or anyone. You will be okay, Gia. Your son or daughter will be okay, too. And he or she will help you find that strength."

"I hope so. I hope you're right."

"But you know what else you have that I didn't?"

I wiped my eyes. "What?"

"You have me. I'll help you, okay? Even if I have to retire a little earlier than planned…I'll make sure you and my grandkid will be okay. So don't be scared."

Raising my voice, I said, "It's not your responsibility."

"You *are* my responsibility, my purpose. You always will be. I don't care how old you are."

Tears were pouring down my face. "I can't tell you how much that means to me to have your support. I've been so scared to tell you. And now with the latest news…I was just so ashamed."

"Don't ever be ashamed to talk to me. You can tell me anything. I'm glad you didn't wait any longer." He placed his hand on mine. "Do you want me to come with you when you tell Rush?"

It was nice of him to offer, but it wouldn't have helped. "No. I have to face this on my own."

"I really like him, Gia. He seems like a really good guy. I hate that this happened."

"You know one of the things I love about Rush…is that he makes me feel protected like you always do. I know that if this hadn't happened, he would have been the best father to this child, whether he realizes it or not. It wouldn't matter that it wasn't his; this baby would've become his in every sense of the word."

"You're talking about things like there is no chance of him sticking around."

I refused to allow myself to feel hopeful. "Do you really think he could possibly handle this?"

Dad let out a long breath and pondered my question. "I think it's going to be very difficult for him. *Very* difficult. And it's gonna take a long time to absorb. But I wouldn't disregard his feelings for you. And I wouldn't rule out the possibility of ending up with him. The bottom line is…you didn't know about his brother. He can't blame you…because you just didn't know. You didn't choose this."

I hated that he was trying to get my hopes up because my gut told me there was no way in hell Rush could ever accept this scenario.

"I wouldn't be able to handle it if the situation were reversed. If I had a sister and he'd gotten her pregnant, there would be no way I could raise that baby. It would just be too painful. So I shouldn't expect him to accept it, either." I sniffled and wiped my eyes again. "You know…I thought my biggest problem was the pregnancy…but I've been growing accustomed to the idea of motherhood, even getting excited over it. And that was all because of him…because I had his support. This twist of fate blindsided me, and now…I just can't see the future anymore at all, at least not one that includes him in it."

He pulled me into his arms. "You can't live like this. Promise me you'll tell him as soon as you get back. Get it over with, Gia. It's not going to get any easier."

It was dark and raining on the ride home. Appropriate weather for my mood. Rush had rented me a reliable vehicle again for my ride to the City. I dialed him from the car on the way home.

He picked up. "Hey, baby. Are you on the road? You shouldn't be talking when you're driving."

"I have you on speaker. It's okay."

"It's raining there, huh?"

"Yeah. Pretty heavily."

"Be careful."

"I will. Don't worry."

"How did the visit with your dad go?"

I exhaled. "Surprisingly good, actually."

"He took the news okay?"

"Yeah…as well as could be expected."

"God, that's a relief. Must be a load off your chest."

If he only knew the weight of the load on my chest right now. Talking to my father had just made the burden heavier since he told me not to wait to tell Rush. I closed my eyes briefly to curb the tears that were forming. If only telling my father about the pregnancy was the only hurdle I had to get through this week.

"You want me to come over tonight or are you tired?" he asked.

"I think I'm gonna go straight to bed. I'm super exhausted."

"Be careful driving if you're sleepy. Pull over if you have to. Get a hotel. I'll give you my credit card. I don't want you to—"

"Rush…" I interrupted.

"Yeah…"

I forced the words out. "There's something I need to talk to you about. Tomorrow. It's too late tonight, but can you come over after work?"

He sounded alarmed. "What's going on, Gia?"

"I can't talk about it over the phone, okay? I love you, Rush. It has nothing to do with my feelings for you or anything. Just something important."

"I'm supposed to be heading into the City for a business meeting tomorrow. Want me to cancel it?"

"No." I insisted, needing as much time as possible to prepare. "Don't do that. Just come over right after. Okay?"

There was a long moment of silence before he answered, "Okay."

CHAPTER 4

Rush

Nothing was going to ruin my mood today.

I waited for the woman behind the counter to finish her phone call and looked around at the portraits hanging on the wall. If stumbling onto this place hadn't been a sign from up above, I didn't know what was.

"Sorry about that." The woman hung up the phone and walked over to where I stood.

"No problem. I didn't have an appointment or anything. I was just on my way to a meeting down the block, and the photos hanging in your window caught my eye. Are you the photographer?"

The woman reminded me of my mom. She was tiny, with long, flowing, dirty blonde hair and a Stevie Nicks vibe. "Yes. They're all mine. This is my portrait studio. I'm sort of a one-woman show—answer the phones, take the photos, print them, and frame them. I can't help myself. I'm a control freak."

"Well, that seems to work for you. They're incredible."

She smiled warmly. "Thank you. Were you looking for a particular type of shoot? Is it for yourself? Or a family portrait of some kind?"

"I'd like to schedule a shoot for someone…as a gift. My girlfriend…something like this, maybe." I pointed to the oversized, framed photo of a very pregnant woman looking down at her exposed belly. She had one hand covering her breasts and the other caressing her stomach. It was beautiful—the quality and softness of the shot gave it an almost angelic feel. "She's been a little down lately, and I think she's getting self-conscious about her body. I want her to see herself like I see her."

"Oh, that's wonderful. What a nice surprise. Many women don't feel so beautiful about their bodies when they're pregnant. You giving her something like this tells her that you're proud of her body and she should be, too."

"That's what I'm hoping. She's gorgeous pregnant."

"Do you have an idea of when you want to bring her in? Let me get my calendar, and I can show you some packages. I'll be right back."

My eyes moved to the framed portrait next to the one of the pregnant woman. The two photos on the wall were the same ones that hung in the window and caught my attention from the street. It was the combination that stopped me in my tracks on the way to my meeting. Next to the pregnant woman was a large portrait of a baby. She was probably only a few months old and sound asleep with her little ass sticking straight in the air while she lay on a white, furry blanket. Her knees were tucked under her tiny body, and her chubby cheeks rested atop her hands as she slept. But the thing that stopped me was *the wings*. The sleeping angel had a set of white, feathery wings on her back. She truly looked like an angel.

"I'm Jenny, by the way. I probably should have opened with that before."

I extended my hand. "Rush. Nice to meet you, Jenny."

When she opened her calendar, every page had scribble all over it. She was pretty damn booked up.

"Looks like you're busy."

"Don't worry. I'll fit you in whenever you want it. Any man who thinks his pregnant partner looks good enough to want to buy her a photoshoot takes priority in my book."

She didn't know the half of it. *Looks good enough.* I wanted to devour Gia twenty-four seven. And you could bet I'd be getting a few extra copies of the shots for myself. Jenny might not think I was so sweet if I told her I wanted duplicates for future spank bank material.

"Thank you. I appreciate that."

"So, all of my packages come with a one-hour photo session. A few days after the shoot, I send you a link to the photos, and you pick which photos you want to have printed. I have packages that range from two photo selections up to eight."

I scratched at the scruff on my chin and looked at the portraits again. "Do you have any packages that include two shoots? I'm thinking I'd like to buy one for my girlfriend now and one for the baby when he's born."

"I do. I have a package that includes two sessions with ten photo selections, and you can pick your ten shots from a combination of both shoots."

"I'll take that one."

Jenny smiled. "Your girlfriend is a lucky girl."

"Trust me. I'm the lucky one."

I actually fucking whistled walking from the photography studio to my meeting, even though I was about to be in the company of my father and brother. Jenny had given me a little bag with a gift certificate inside and a tiny, golden angel trinket. It couldn't have been more perfect. I hoped Gia liked the present as much as I knew I would.

My whistle cut mid-stream when my brother walked into the elevator. We had a meeting up on the thirty-third floor with our banker and some people about a potential investment. Elliott flashed a phony smile and turned to give me his back as the car doors slid closed. "I have a good tailor who can make you a nice suit." He buttoned his overpriced suit jacket as he spoke. "If you'd like, I can send you his number."

Today I'd worn a dress shirt and slacks, in deference to Robert Harmon, the banker with whom we were meeting. He was a good friend of our grandfather's and deserved the respect of putting on something decent. My asshole brother, on the other hand, deserved nothing.

"Unlike you, I don't have to drop a load of cash to like myself when I look in the mirror. A personality and tact is a fuck of a lot cheaper than four grand for a suit."

Elliott snickered. "I'd love to spend this quality time trading jabs with my bastard brother, but we actually have business we should discuss before we arrive upstairs." I watched him wipe some lint off the front of his jacket in the reflection of the shiny metal doors before continuing. "This isn't just the annual meeting with Robert. We need him to increase our business line of credit for this investment."

"For what?"

He sighed. "A hotel in Costa Rica."

My forehead wrinkled. "A what?"

"There's a property that's come available for sale in Costa Rica. It's priced way below market value and it's a great investment. Two of the owners who are selling it have come up to talk to us. They'll give you and Robert the dog and pony show."

"Okay…so why do you need to involve me at all? You want to invest, invest."

"We need an increase to our business line of credit to help purchase the property. Which means our little family corporation needs a resolution vote for the increase in our credit line."

"Why do you need a line of credit business loan? Get a mortgage on the property like you would any other building."

"It needs to be an all cash deal. No mortgage."

"Why?"

"Because that's what the seller wants. He's already got another offer. But he'll take ours for the same price. It's a once-in-a-lifetime opportunity. Costa Rica is a growing tourist market."

"What do you even know about running a hotel?"

"There's staff. But I'll spend a lot of time down there making sure things are taken care of properly."

"Let me guess? Your wife will stay up here in New York. It'll be like your own little vacation fuck paradise. No thanks."

The doors slid open, and my brother turned to face me. "Listen to the presentation today before you make any hasty decision. You'll see. It's almost too good to be true."

I shook my head and stepped off the elevator before my brother, stopping to look back at him. "You know what they say about things that seem too good to be true? *They probably are*."

Something didn't add up. Two of the owners made an hour-and-a-half presentation, yet it seemed more like a timeshare sales pitch for a vacation resort than any business proposal. The hotel was nice. There was no denying that. But I couldn't grasp two important things: why they would sell it if it were such a profitable business, and why the purchase couldn't have a mortgage.

"The place is beautiful. But I have a couple of questions."

My father and brother made a face.

"Shoot," said the owner, who'd done most of the talking. "We're here to answer whatever questions you have."

"Alright. Edward and Elliott are interested in the property. I'm not interested in taking over something that I know nothing about."

My brother mumbled, "That never stopped you before."

I didn't even turn my head to acknowledge Elliott. "Anyway. It's my understanding that this deal has to be a cash deal, rather than a mortgage. Which means the financing would be a business line of credit—which, in turn, means my interest in Vanderhaus Holdings is on the hook for this venture, as well. So I'd like to understand why the property can't be mortgaged."

The two men looked at each other and then to Elliott. It was my brother who answered my question. "There are a few investor-owners who prefer a discreet transaction. They're not listed on the legal documents as owners. And then there's a small issue with the IRS for one of the listed investors."

I narrowed my eyes. "How small?"

One of the two selling investors responded. "The transaction needs to be cash, or the funds are going to be confiscated by the government because of a tax judgment. Don't worry…the Costa Rica property itself doesn't have any liens. Just one of our investors."

Did my brother ever get involved in anything that wasn't shady as shit?

I kept quiet after that. My decision had been made. I'm all for stretching the truth on my business mileage and office expenses when it came to my taxes, but I wasn't about to get involved with any major cash transactions that were structured to avoid someone paying taxes on their IRS lien, and God knows the reason the other investors needed a *discreet* transaction.

Our meeting ended, and the two hotel owners said goodbye. Robert, our banker, stuck around to chat with Edward, leaving me with my jackass brother. Robert had put some forms in the middle of the table that we would all need to sign to increase our line of credit with the bank by millions of dollars.

Elliott slipped a pen from inside his jacket pocket and flung it across the table at me. "Why don't you sign now, so you can be on your merry way?"

"I'm not signing this thing." I slid the pen that had landed in front of me to the middle of the table. "I may not know too much about business, but I know a shady deal when I see one. This is exactly the type of thing that Grandfather wouldn't go near with a ten-foot pole."

My brother's face contorted. "Stop being so naïve, and just sign the fucking thing. It's a good investment. You'll never have to pay a dime out of pocket toward the loan payments. Profits will cover everything."

"I don't think it's a wise decision to put all of the other Vanderhaus businesses at risk for a single hotel in Costa

Rica. First, you don't know anything about running a hotel. And, second, there's something shady about the deal. The owners just flat out told you that they need cash because they are trying to avoid paying a tax lien. Think they're going to be any more honest with you than the government?"

Elliott stood. His chair tumbled over from the way he whipped from the table so fast. He raised his voice. "It's not bad enough we have to share profits with you, now you're interfering with us making them. You should appreciate that you even get anything from us."

"I think you're forgetting that I don't get anything from *you*. Our grandfather left me the shares in *his* company. If you weren't so spoiled and entitled, you'd see there is a difference."

"You're just being vindictive. Isn't it about time that you accept that your family will always take sloppy seconds from the Vanderhaus men?"

I stood. "Fuck you."

Elliott fiddled with his expensive watch. "Your little trashy girlfriend wasn't even that good of a lay anyway."

My blood started to pump. I had to have misheard him. "What the hell did you just say?"

"I didn't even remember that I'd tapped that until she reminded me at my party." He shook his head. "Forgettable."

I slammed both fists on the table and leaned across it toward my brother. "What *the fuck* are you talking about, asshole?"

Elliott looked back and forth between my rage-filled eyes. An evil sneer that gave me chills spread across his face. He tilted his head. "She didn't tell you, did she?"

"Tell me what?"

It was one thing for him to insult my business acumen and me personally, but I'd be damned if this asshole was going to say shit about Gia. I was barely able to contain myself.

He tsked. "It must be a Rushmore genetic trait. First your mother tried to take what my mother already had. And now you're banging one of my leftovers."

I jumped onto and over the table faster than Elliott could even move. The smirk still didn't fall from his face when I pushed him up against the wall and pressed my forearm to his throat. Edward and Robert tried to rip me off of him, but I didn't budge.

"Don't you even say Gia's name. She wouldn't give you the time of day."

The asshole started to turn red, yet somehow he managed to speak. "She gave me the time of day alright. Twice that night, if I remember correctly. I really liked the cute little heart-shaped mole on her ass when I had her on all fours."

I suddenly felt like I was the one being choked. My grip loosened a little, not because I wanted to let him breathe, but because I couldn't breathe now. Elliott was able to take advantage of my shock and pushed my arm from his throat.

He coughed while I stood there frozen. There was no fucking way Gia had slept with my brother. She'd never do that to me. There had to be another way he knew about the heart-shaped mole.

Edward put his arm around his son and scowled at me. "You're really an animal." He looked to Elliott. "Are you alright?"

"Yeah." His voice was hoarse from almost having his windpipe crushed. He looked at me and gave one last vicious smile. "Tell your girlfriend that Harlan said hello."

CHAPTER 5

Rush

No fucking answer. *Again.*

I tossed my cell onto the wooden bar and waved down the bartender.

"Another Vodka and 7."

"Bad day at work?" he asked while making me a third drink.

"You could say that."

"What do you do?"

"I have some businesses with my estranged family."

The guy chuckled and slid my drink across the bar. "This one's on the house. Couldn't pay me to work with my family."

I should've driven home after leaving the office. But instead, I found the nearest dive bar and parked myself on a stool. Now it was four o'clock in the afternoon, and I was halfway loaded and more than a hundred-plus miles from Gia, who wasn't picking up the fucking phone.

I downed half my drink in one gulp. Cheap vodka. Tomorrow I'd pay for it.

A million fucking scenarios had played through my head over the last hour. Maybe he was full of shit—somehow he'd found out that information about Gia and used it to piss me off. Gia could have chatted with Lauren at the party for a little while, and I hadn't noticed. Maybe she'd mentioned she was pregnant with some guy named Harlan's baby. And Lauren had told her husband.

It could happen.

Although I had a more difficult time explaining how *the fuck* he knew about the heart-shaped mole on her ass.

I squeezed the glass in my hand so tight, I thought it might crack. The thought of Elliott knowing firsthand about Gia's mole made me want to explode.

There were a dozen other scenarios that I came up with. None of them pretty.

Gia must've known who I was from the start. She'd slept with my brother and then set her sights on me to get even with Elliott for screwing her over and leaving her pregnant. *That just isn't possible. This was Gia, for Christ's sake.*

Gia and Elliott are still sleeping together.

Gia was a plant by Elliott and Edward to try and distract me.

My mind seemed to be running rampant, and the more I sipped my drink, the wilder the scenarios that I imagined.

The entire thing just needed to be wrong somehow. There was a logical explanation for this. I needed to just calm the fuck down. Once I finally got through to Gia, she'd make sense of it all.

Yet, I couldn't stop myself from going over and over how Gia had described Harlan over the last two months.

Well-dressed—looked like the typical Hampton crowd.

Elliott *was* the typical Hampton-looking douche.

Articulate and put together.

My brother may be a dick, but he was well-educated and put on a good front.

She'd met him at The Heights.

Elliott *had* come around a few times when I wasn't there earlier in the summer. My staff had told me about it the next day.

Not to mention, now that I think about it, *Harlan* was my father's dog's name growing up. That fact had completely slipped my mind even though the afternoon I first saw that dog was clear as day in my mind right now.

I was probably eleven or twelve, and my mother had taken me to visit my grandfather. It was the week before Christmas, and he had the biggest damn tree I'd ever seen set up next to the fireplace in his living room. Trains were set up around the thing. Grandfather had told me there was a remote for the trains up on the mantel and that I could play with them while he and my mom talked in the other room. When I went to grab it, I'd found a framed family portrait on display next to the remote. A portrait of my father's family. It was like some shit out of *The Waltons*—everyone had plastic smiles. The mom was sitting in a fancy chair, the dad stood behind her with one hand on her shoulder, and the boy was down on one knee next to a golden retriever. I remember thinking they could sell this shit as the picture that comes inside the frames at the store. As much as I hated it, I also couldn't stop staring at it. I never did wind up playing with the trains, but when Grandfather came back—I still had the framed photo in my hand, and I asked what the dog's name was.

Harlan.

That's what he'd said.

How the fuck had I forgotten that until now?

46

I guess I had no reason to suspect anything. Or maybe I was just too blinded by a set of great tits and a gorgeous ass to see anything that was staring me straight in the face.

Dumb fuck I am.

I sucked back the rest of my drink and started to feel numb. That's exactly what I needed. To get the thoughts in my head drunk enough to stop them for a little while.

"Is this seat taken?" A woman sidled up next to me.

I waved toward a dozen empty chairs alongside the one she had in her hand. "Looks like you have your choice of seats."

She batted her eyelashes. "Good. I choose this one."

My new neighbor waved down the bartender and decided we were going to be friends. "I'm Amanda."

"Rush." I nodded, keeping my head forward.

"Are you from around here? I don't think I've seen you in here before."

"Nope."

The bartender walked over, and she pointed to my drink. "I'll have one of whatever he's having."

"You sure?" he asked. "That's pretty much a glass of vodka with a splash of 7 Up."

"I'm sure. I had a bad day. And give my new friend Rush a refill, too." She slid a fifty-dollar bill onto the bar. "On me."

I put my hand out. "Thanks, but I'll cover my own drink."

I caught her pout out of the corner of my eye.

"I wasn't asking you to marry me," she said. "It was just a drink. You look like you've had a bad day, too. Figured we could commiserate together."

Now I felt like a dick. I looked at the bartender. "Put hers on my tab, please."

Amanda smiled. "Thank you."

I nodded.

Neither of us spoke again until after the bartender delivered our drinks. She took one sip and crinkled up her nose. "This is strong."

"Yep."

"Wanna play a game?"

My eyes flashed to hers and back. "Nope."

More pouting. "Come on. I can tell we both had a shitty day. Let's compare shitty days, and the one who had a worse shitty day has to pay for the drinks today."

"No thanks," I said.

"Alright then…I'll start…"

I shook my head, but it didn't stop her flapping her mouth.

"Well…I work at Forever 21…you know…the clothes store. I was up for a promotion to be assistant manager, and my boss gave it to Tatia—some new girl who's only worked there for two months. I've been working there for two years and only called in sick twice. She's been there for a couple of months and already took as many days off. So I got upset and went to McDonald's at lunch—where I proceed to eat a Big Mac *and* a cheeseburger, along with a large fries and a Coke—not even a Diet Coke. When I went back to work, I decided I was going to talk to the manager and find out why I didn't get the promotion I was supposed to get. But when I went into the back office, I found out the reason without him saying a word. Tatia was on his lap riding him on the chair. The bitch smiled at me when I caught them and went right back to playing cowgirl."

For the first time, I looked over at Amanda. My first assessment was—if she eats when she's stressed, she must not get upset too often. Amanda was damn cute—the kind of woman I was normally attracted to. Lots of makeup and dark hair, a low-cut shirt that showed off big tits and a short skirt that gave a lot of leg.

"That sucks," I said.

A smile spread across her face and she clapped. "Free drinks for me!"

I shook my head, lifted my fourth vodka to my lips, and sucked back a heaping gulp. "My girlfriend is pregnant with my brother's baby."

Her jaw dropped. "Oh my God. Are you kidding me?"

I rattled around the ice in my glass. "Nope."

She opened her purse and dug out a credit card. Putting it on the bar, she said, "Drinks on me."

———

We were shitfaced.

Amanda turned out to be pretty cool, and it felt good to unload all of the crazy shit in my head to a stranger. I'd always been the type of guy to think people who went to shrinks were pussies—couldn't suck it up and handle their own problems. But I was definitely starting to see that purging, instead of bottling up all that shit, could have its advantages.

"My high school boyfriend fucked my best friend."

"That's pretty bad," I said.

She deadpanned. "My best friend was *Darren*."

We both cracked up. Over the last hour, we had ruminated over crappy things that happened in our lives, telling each other random stories of screwed-up things we'd experienced. I was pretty sure that we were both slurring our words, maybe even talking in our own drunken language that no one else could understand. But it was my turn for a shitty story, so I sucked back a healthy gulp.

"When I was thirteen, I got head for the first time—from my best friend's sixteen-year-old sister. I was too young to control myself and finished off in her mouth. She wasn't happy about it, so she told my best friend that I'd hit on her and grabbed her ass, even though she'd been the one to come onto me. He decided we had to fist fight about it. I was in the wrong, so I let the skinny little shit give me a black eye and bloody nose thinking that would make him feel like he evened the score and we could go back to being buddies. Didn't work. I lost my best friend because of a blow job."

Amanda laughed. "Have you learned how to control yourself better yet?"

"That shit traumatized me. Damn straight I never made that mistake again. You gotta get permission. *Don't blow till you know*. That's been my motto the last sixteen years."

Amanda almost fell off her chair laughing so hard. We'd been having a good time, like two guys comparing war stories. Only Amanda definitely wasn't a guy. That fact became suddenly clear when she rested her hand on my thigh. "For the record, I'd be okay with you losing control."

Fuck.

This conversation suddenly went from innocent to feeling really fucking wrong. I looked down at her hand on my thigh and then up into the eyes of my new friend. "I fucking love her."

She gave a sad smile. "I know. But if you wanted to maybe get even…I only live a few blocks from here."

I shook my head. "I can't."

"You sure? No strings attached. It might be good to let out all of our anger." She leaned in and whispered, "I like it a little rough." Then she stood. "Think about it. I'm going to go to the ladies' room."

I like it a little rough.

Fuck.

I finished my drink and told the bartender to put both our tabs on my card, instead of Amanda's. While I was digging my wallet from my pocket, my phone started to buzz on the bar. Gia's name flashed, and my heart started to race. *Finally.* I abruptly felt sober. I swiped to answer.

"Where the fuck have you been all day? I've been trying to call you for hours," I barked into the phone.

"I'm sorry. I fell asleep because I was up sick last night."

I pushed aside the ache in my chest from hearing she wasn't feeling good. "Who's the damn father of your baby, Gia?"

"What?" It only took her saying one word to hear the nerves fray in her voice.

I yelled louder, "Who the fuck is the father, Gia?"

Silence.

"Answer me, goddamn it!"

Her voice shook. "Rush. Let's talk about this when you get home. Remember, we are supposed to talk tonight?"

"Who. The. Fuck. Is. The. Father. Gia?

She started to cry. But I couldn't feel bad. I needed to hear her say it.

"Answer me."

"I can't!"

"Did you fuck my brother?"

Sobbing.

"Goddamn it, Gia. Answer me. Are you pregnant with that piece of shit's spawn?"

"I'm so sorry," she cried. "I didn't know until the birthday party. I was planning on telling you tonight. I'm so, so sorry."

"Say it. Say the words, Gia. I need to fucking hear them."

"Please, Rush. Where are you? We need to talk about this in person. I'll come to you. Are you home?"

"Say it!" The sadistic bastard in me needed to hear it.

"I can't."

"I *need* to fucking hear it, Gia. I'm not fucking around. *Say it.*"

She sniffled, and the words were barely a whisper. But she said it. The words that shattered my fucking heart into a million pieces.

"Elliott is the father of my baby."

CHAPTER 6

Gia

So began what was very likely the worst night of my entire life.

Rush had hung up distraught after my revelation. I couldn't say I blamed him. It was exactly the reaction I'd expected.

The hours that followed were pure torture. I was worried. Really worried about him. And the fact that I couldn't reach him to confirm that he was okay wasn't helping.

Finding out through Elliott was the worst possible scenario. His brother had no idea what news he was *really* giving Rush. I assumed he had no clue I was carrying his baby. Finding out I had slept with Elliott would have been terrible news in and of itself. But for Rush to have received the news in such a cold way, knowing what it really meant, was simply cruel.

I was up most of the night dialing him, to no avail. He just wouldn't answer. When I finally accepted the fact that maybe he needed some time apart from me to process everything, I tried to force myself to sleep for a bit, even though it was extremely difficult to relax. My tired body eventually succumbed to slumber, and I ended up getting a couple of hours of sleep.

When I woke up, the birds were chirping, and the sun was starting to rise. It couldn't have been more than 6AM. Someone was downstairs brewing coffee, and the smell was making me nauseous.

My heart was palpitating as I urgently reached for my phone to call him again. Still no answer. I tried again.

Come on, Rush. Answer.

It just went to voicemail again. Starting to panic, I decided to throw some clothes on and drive to his house.

When I arrived, the ocean was choppy and the wind was fierce. It was fitting for the tumultuous mood of this morning. The wind chimes that were hanging near his front door were working overtime to keep up.

Rush usually parked in the driveway, but it was empty. I peeked inside the small windows at the top of the garage door. His car wasn't there, either.

Where is he?

I wasn't sure if I really wanted to know, although a part of me *needed* to know the answer.

Had he never come home last night?

Maybe he'd gotten drunk and left his car somewhere? Maybe someone else drove him home? I knocked repeatedly on the front door.

Nothing.

He definitely wasn't home.

Returning to my car parked outside, I picked up my phone and dialed him once again.

To my shock, this time someone answered. But it wasn't Rush.

"Hello?"

It was a woman with a groggy voice. My heart started to beat faster.

"Who is this?" I said.

She repeated my question. "Who is *this*?"

"It's Gia. Where's Rush?"

"Gia? Gia! The woman who fucked Rush's brother? Wow. Why are you even calling him? You've got some nerve."

My heart sank. I tasted the bile rising from my stomach, feeling a bit betrayed that he would spill our business to some slut he just met.

"Who is this? Where is Rush?"

"You're a real piece of work. You lost a good one, bitch."

"Excuse me?"

There was no response. Then the phone went dead in my ear. She'd hung up on me.

My car shook from the wind. Resting my head against the steering wheel, I wanted to cry, but the shock from what just happened must have dried my tears.

He was with a woman.

The realization of that felt like a death had occurred. As hard as it was to accept, I couldn't even be mad at him. I was sad, but I didn't have the right to be mad. After the horrifying news I'd given him, how could I expect that he'd be able to handle things alone? Yes, I was jealous and sick to my stomach, but a part of me understood.

Shutting my eyes tightly, I tried to shun thoughts of Rush screwing another woman.

I clutched my stomach, looking out toward the house that was once going to be my home. Now it was very likely that my baby would never see the nursery that Rush built. It was just one of the many dreams that had been shattered over one really bad decision.

———

That night, right before I was scheduled to work, I stood outside The Heights, hesitant to go in. He might have been in there. Would he face me or continue to ignore me? How would I feel looking at him after knowing he'd been with another woman? So many questions flew in and out of my brain. My heart was pummeling against my chest. God, this level of stress could not have been good for my baby.

I didn't feel prepared to handle any of this. But honestly, I had no choice but to work tonight. The fact of the matter was, at the moment, I had no other job, no money, and a baby on the way. That reminded me that I really needed to make finding another job a priority before I moved back to the City.

Taking a deep breath in, I made my way toward the door and entered.

Oak was standing near the hostess station, looking like he might have been waiting for me.

"Hi," I said.

He seemed anxious. "Hey, Gia."

I swallowed. "Is Rush here?"

"Boss is in his office. I don't know what's going on. He wouldn't talk to me, but he doesn't look good. In fact, I've never seen him like this. Looks like he got run over by a truck and smells like he got thrown in a bar dumpster. You may want to go in and check on him."

My heart sank. "How long has he been here?"

"Hours. He hasn't come out and he yelled at me a few times to leave him alone."

I expelled a long breath. "I'm pretty sure that I'm the last person he wants to see right now, Oak."

Oak nodded in understanding. "Oh…okay, so this has something to do with you guys. That's what I was afraid of." He frowned. "I'm sorry to hear that."

"Yeah. I think it might be best if I let him come out on his own. He knows I'm working. I think he'll seek me out when he's ready. I'm afraid to make him more upset."

He looked around and lowered his voice. "Can I ask what happened?"

I simply shook my head no. Thankfully, he didn't push it.

My shift that night was excruciating. I couldn't go two minutes without looking down the hallway to see if Rush was going to come out of his office. He never did. I even passed by a few times and placed my ear on the door to see if I could hear anything. And nothing. I was starting to think that maybe he'd snuck out during one of the few times I was too preoccupied to notice.

At the end of the night, I just couldn't take it anymore. I had cash to put in the safe, so I figured that was a good 'official' excuse to enter his office.

When I opened the door with the money in hand, the lights were off. I assumed he'd left until his voice shook me to my core.

"Who's there?"

I froze. "It's me. I have cash for the safe."

"Leave it on the desk," he demanded coldly.

I stood there in the dark. The door was halfway open, so the only light streaming into the room was from the hallway.

"Are you okay?" I finally asked.

"No."

The pain in his voice was palpable. I wanted so badly to approach him, to hold him, but I knew that wasn't an option. I knew he'd push me away. So I stayed where I was near the door.

"I know you're not ready to talk to me. But I need you to know that I fully intended to tell you. I was still absorbing it myself. I'm so sorry you had to find out through him. I would do anything to take that back. I—"

"Gia…" His curt tone sliced through me. "I can't do this right now. Do you understand? I wish I was stronger for you, but right now, I'm just not." He repeated, "I can't do this."

Tears were starting to form in my eyes. "What can I do? Please tell me," I begged. "I'll do anything."

He was raking his hands through his hair over and over. I hated to think where those hands had been last night.

"You can't, Gia," he finally said. "There is nothing you can do to change this. I just need time."

"Time for what? Is there even a decision to make?"

"I don't know. Like I said…I just can't…"

I wanted to ask him where he was last night and who that woman was, but I refrained even though my curiosity was killing me. It was neither the time nor place to bring even more drama into an already fucked-up situation. He was hurting, and that was what was important, not my feelings of jealousy.

"Rush, I'm going through the same pain that you are."

"I know that. And I wish I could be there for you. I know this isn't easy for you, either. But Gia, I'm ready to fucking kill someone. I can't control my anger right now and it's just best if…" His words dropped off. I couldn't see him clearly, but his shoulders shook. I was pretty sure he was crying.

My heart was breaking. I loved this man with all of my being. To watch him cry and not be able to do anything about it – and to know I had caused it – was just about the most painful feeling I'd ever experienced. I was afraid I'd make it worse if I touched him, and I refused to cause him any more pain.

After some silence where I just listened to him breathe, he finally said, "I just can't handle talking about this until my head is on straight again."

I wiped my eyes. "Okay." I walked over to the desk and placed the money down. Clenching my fists, I once again had to restrain myself from reaching for him. I walked back toward the door but lingered there.

His next words really caught me off guard. "I need to leave town for a while."

My heartbeat sped up.

He was leaving?

My eyes widened. "Leave town?"

"Yes."

"Where are you going?"

"I don't know yet—somewhere to try to clear my head. I'm leaving Oak in charge of The Heights."

"Will you keep in touch while you're away?"

"Don't worry about me. Just take care of yourself…and the baby."

Should I have been pushing harder to break through the walls he'd put up? My gut told me that there was nothing I could do to stop him, that there was no way to solve this through talking. I didn't want to push him over the edge. So I decided to give him the time and space to deal with this. My heart was telling me to let him go.

So that's exactly what I did.

CHAPTER 7

Rush

Everyone was long gone, and I was still sitting in my dark office.

I was glad she listened to me and left, because I seriously couldn't handle being around her yet.

I still loved her so much. That never changed for one second. I just didn't know how to handle what I was feeling, couldn't articulate my pain. And I certainly couldn't make any decisions about my future in this state of mind.

The truth was, I had no idea where to go from here. As much as I felt like I could never abandon Gia, I also felt like I might never be able to accept things as they were.

Accepting the baby as my own when its father was a faceless, nameless phantom was one thing. Accepting the baby as my own knowing that the father is my own brother— arguably my biggest enemy—was a completely different story.

The fact that I couldn't force myself to stay and deal with this was pissing me the fuck off. I'd never been one to run away from my problems. But it just felt like the only option right now. My anger ran too deep to be around her, and I sure as hell needed to be far enough away from Elliott for a while to curb my murderous urges.

It was the middle of the night now as I forced myself out of my chair and out to the parking lot. My plan was to get some shut-eye then pack a bag in the morning and go wherever the wind took me.

Halfway home, my phone rang. I assumed it was Gia calling to check on me.

But it wasn't.

The name on the caller ID was definitely not who I was expecting.

Beth.

Beth?

Beth was my best friend growing up, until I ruined things by sleeping with her. We still kept in touch from time to time after she moved to Arizona, but why would she be calling me at this time of night? *Very odd.*

I picked up. "Beth?"

"Heath. I'm sorry to be calling you so late."

"What's up?"

There was a long pause before she said, "My dad. Heath…he died today. It just happened earlier tonight. He collapsed after dinner in front of the television. Massive heart attack. I've been calling all of our friends and family."

"Oh my God." I immediately pulled over onto a dirt road and placed my hand on my forehead. "Are you okay?"

"We're all pretty shaken up. I think I'm just still in shock. It happened so fast."

"How's your mother?"

"Devastated."

Beth's dad, Pat, had been like a father to me growing up. This news was jarring and couldn't have come at a worse time. I'd already felt like my world had completely fallen apart, but apparently there was still room for more devastation.

"Shit, Beth. I don't even know what to say. I'm so sorry."

"I figured you'd want to know. You guys were so close at one time. And I know he'd want me to reach out to you."

"I wish I even had the right words right now. Nothing I can say is gonna help."

She was crying. "Just hearing your voice helps."

"When is the service?"

"We haven't gotten that far yet, but probably sometime in the next few days."

Suddenly, I didn't have to wonder where I was going anymore.

I was headed to Arizona.

———

It felt surreal walking into the funeral home and seeing Pat Hurley lying there in a coffin. I hadn't seen him in years but we always kept in touch, mainly during the holidays. Now I was feeling guilty that we hadn't communicated more. I would regret not calling him more often for as long as I lived.

As a kid with no father around, you appreciated attention from adult males more than average; yearned for it, even. Pat knew I needed guidance, and he became that father figure to me.

He was the one who taught me how to throw a football, how to fish, and gave me the good old 'birds and the bees' talk. The latter would end up being ironic when I ended up fucking his daughter later on. Pat found out about that, too, and kicked my ass. But he still cared about me even after that. He loved me and he never let me forget it, even when he was literally smacking the shit out of me.

I stood by his coffin and stared down at his body. Pat was dressed in a nice suit, and his mouth had been formed into a smile. He looked good for a dead guy. I couldn't even believe I was thinking about Pat that way, or that he was gone forever from this Earth.

God, this sucked. This sucked so freaking bad.

I wiped my eyes and, after saying some prayers, I stood up and looked around. It felt like someone turned the heat up to a hundred degrees. Beads of sweat were forming on my forehead. My tie felt like it was choking me, so I loosened it.

There was a long line of people waiting to give condolences to the family. I stood at the back of it waiting with everyone else.

Beth's mother, Ann, was first in the line-up. I noticed how much she'd aged, but damn, it had been a long time, hadn't it? Over ten years. Beth's brother, Adam, was next to his mother. He had gained some weight.

Beth was standing next to him. I almost didn't recognize her. She looked a lot different. She was never heavy but always had some meat on her. Now she was almost what you'd consider skinny. Her once light brown hair was dyed blonde. She was wearing bright lipstick and a tight black dress. She looked good.

A little boy with long, shaggy hair stood next to her. I knew Beth was married with a son, so I assumed that was him. He had her almond-shaped eyes and looked to be about six.

When I got to Ann, she placed both hands on my cheeks and cried, "Heath…I can't believe you came all this way. I wish Pat were here to see you."

The right words escaped me. I simply said, "I'm so sorry, Ann."

"We're having a family dinner after this. Will you stay and join us?"

"Yeah. I'm gonna stay in town for a little bit."

"Good. I'll see you there."

As I hugged her brother next, I could feel the weight of Beth's eyes on me.

By the time I got to her, it took less than a second for her to pull me into a tight hug.

She was trembling. I felt her hot breath against my skin as she cried into my shoulder.

Her hands gripped my arms as she said, "Heath. You made it. It's so good to see you. You have no idea."

Mascara ran down her face, but the smudges accentuated her bright blue eyes. I'd forgotten how pretty Beth was.

"How are you holding up?" I asked.

"Just floating on through. It still feels surreal."

"I know. I can't even believe that's him over there. It feels like he should be standing right here, smacking me on the back, and swearing at me for not calling him enough."

She cracked a smile. "I'm certain that he's looking down right now and that he's so happy you're here with us."

"I'm happy I'm here, too. I wish it were under different circumstances. But there's nowhere else I belong tonight."

Her gaze lingered on mine before she looked down and reached for the little boy's hand. "Owen, this is Heath. He's one of Mommy's oldest friends."

The boy looked up at me and said, "He's not that old."

I chuckled. "I'm getting there, little dude." Reaching out my hand to him, I said, "It's nice to meet you."

He took it. "You, too."

The line had to keep moving, so I said to her, "I'll see you after."

She grabbed my hand to stop me from leaving. "There's a dinner tonight at the house. Please come."

"Yeah. Your mother mentioned. I'll be there."

"I'll text you the address."

I nodded. "Okay."

———

The Hurley home was a modest, single-family house surrounded by cactus plants in the Arizona desert. It was nothing like the two-family house Beth grew up in on Long Island.

Ann had set up a catered buffet in the dining room and had invited about fifty people back to the house after the wake. Even though the mood was somber, there was a lot of talking. I just wanted some food and to sit down for a bit. It had been a long flight, and I was starting to feel jetlagged. Tomorrow would be an even longer day with the funeral.

Beth's brother was married now, too. His two kids were running around with Owen. Ann was quiet, being consoled by different people on a constant basis. I couldn't imagine how crushed she was. She and Pat had been married for over thirty-five years. They were the perfect example of a loving couple and loving parents. I'd always envied Beth's family.

Pat's passing was such a sad reason to be here, but in a strange way it was probably one of the only things that could've shifted the focus off of my own situation. Death has a way of doing that.

As I took my plate of chicken cordon bleu and rice over to a corner in the living room, I gazed at some of the framed family photos that were sitting on a bookshelf. Man, how I wished I could run my troubles by Pat right now. I wondered how he'd feel about everything, what advice he'd give me. I hadn't ever thought about opening up to him about Gia, mainly because it became a little awkward to talk to him about women after the Beth thing went down. I knew he cared deeply about me, but things definitely changed after I'd broken his daughter's heart before they moved. I would always regret crossing that line in my friendship with her back then, but I couldn't take it back. I was a dumb fucking teenager who couldn't control his dick.

Beth discovered my hiding spot in the corner of the living room. "Hey. There you are. I've been looking for you."

My head was still turned toward the photos. "I was just looking at these photos, thinking about your dad, how lucky I was to have him in my life growing up."

"He loved you like a son. Even after you and I grew apart, he always talked about you, Heath. Always. He really missed you after we moved." She hesitated. "I missed you, too."

I finally looked at her, and our eyes locked. It was really good to see Beth. At one time, she'd been my best friend. In a weird way, in his death, Pat had given me exactly what I needed: a place away from home but with the comfort of familiar faces.

"Hey," I said. "I was gonna ask…if you'd accept my help tomorrow, I'd be honored to be a pallbearer."

"That's really nice of you. I know Daddy would love that. I'll talk to Mom. We can definitely make that happen."

"Thanks. It would really mean a lot to me."

Ann didn't know it yet, but I planned to make arrangements with the funeral home to cover all of the expenses. It was the least I could do for a man who'd given me so much.

Beth took a seat in the chair across from me and crossed her legs. "So tell me what's happening back in New York. The businesses are going okay? Is your brother still an asshole?"

Fuck. Don't bring him up right now. I'm trying to forget. A mental image of Gia fucking him was now infiltrating my mind.

Goddammit. Why wasn't I drinking?

I took a deep breath and literally shook my head to rid myself of the thoughts. "Yeah. Still an asshole."

"I figured." She laughed then changed the subject. "Are you seeing anyone?"

There was no way I was gonna get into everything now. "It's complicated." I loved how those two words just took care of having to explain anything further.

"Ah, okay." She smiled then swirled her drink around in the glass. "How long are you staying in Scottsdale?"

"I'm not sure. At least a week, I think."

"I would love to hang out, catch up."

"Well, I don't know my way around here, so that'd be cool," I said.

"I'm glad you're not taking off so fast."

I looked around the room, wondering why I hadn't been introduced to her husband yet. "Where's your husband? I haven't met him."

"He stopped by the wake before you got there. He came by to drop off Owen."

"He's not here?"

She stared down at her drink. "No."

"Why not?"

Beth looked me in the eyes. "We're not together anymore. We divorced."

CHAPTER 8

Rush

I'd forgotten why we were best friends before I screwed it all up—before either of us noticed that she was a girl and I was a boy, before I became distracted by her perky teenage tits and plump ass. But today had brought it all back.

Beth had taken a week off of work after her father died, so she had plenty of free time to show me around. When I'd arrived at her house to pick her up for our day of sightseeing, she said that she'd arranged for her neighbor to babysit Owen. But after finding out that she was divorced yesterday, it felt wrong to spend the day alone with her. Friend or not, things between me and Gia were unsettled, and I wouldn't be too happy if she spent our time apart sightseeing with a guy she had slept with—especially one as hot as Beth looked in her little shorts and belly-bearing tank top today. So I insisted that Owen come on our sightseeing adventure. At first, I could see that she looked disappointed. She'd probably been looking forward to an adult day out. But after I showed Owen a picture of one of the things I wanted to do today, he was so excited, she couldn't possibly turn either of us down.

The three of us drove two hours to Sedona to see the Red Rocks. I'd called ahead to reserve two ATVs, one with a cage around it that would be safer for Owen and one regular, open-air-style quad. Of course, I'd assumed I'd be driving the one without the safety roll cage. I'd forgotten the wild streak in Beth.

Our guide came to show us how to use the machines and then gave us all helmets. Beth hopped onto the ATV without the roll cage.

"What do you think you're doing?" I asked.

She jumped on the kickstart, and the loud roar of the engine came to life. "I'm about to kick your butt, that's what I'm doing," she yelled.

"Don't you think the roll cage would be safer for Owen?"

"I'm not driving Owen. He and I together would probably be closer to what you weigh. I need to keep my weight light to win this race."

I furrowed my brows. "What race?"

She smirked. "Remember the bet we had when we were ten? I'd just gotten that new blue Schwinn, and I challenged you to a race up to old man Caulfield's house. You'd beaten me every damn race we ever had, and I thought for sure my new bike would give me the edge I needed."

I vaguely remembered it. The only part that was clear in my head was that I'd smoked her. New bicycle or not, her chicken legs back then didn't have a shot against my thick ones. "I won. Of course." I turned to Owen and bragged. "Your mother and I used to compete at everything. I always won. You know why?"

He had the best goofy grin. "Why?"

"Because girls go to Jupiter to get more stupider; boys go to college to get more knowledge."

Owen found it amusing, while Beth rolled her eyes. "Don't listen to Heath, Owen. He can't even remember the old saying. It's *boys* go to Jupiter to get more stupider, *girls* go to college to get more knowledge." She squinted at me. "You made me eat an ant and a dead moth. Remember?"

I laughed. I'd forgotten that we used to bet bug eating as the prize. Winner got to pick one bug for the other person to eat. But she had been so sure that her new, fancy bike would carry her ass to victory, she'd doubled down our usual bet.

"Mom ate bugs? She won't even eat a fish unless it's cut up so you don't see the head and eyes and stuff."

"Your mother was a tomboy. She could climb a tree, skim a rock, and throw a spiral better than any of the boys." I leaned to Owen and winked. "Except me, of course."

Beth pulled on her helmet. "Losers eat THREE bugs. And, beware, Rushmore, the bugs in Arizona require a fork and a knife."

Before I could argue anymore, she hit the gas and took off.

"You scared to get in that thing, buddy?" I lifted my chin to the ATV.

"Heck, no. Let's kick Mom's butt!"

———

"You cheated."

I looked at my partner in crime. "In order to cheat, we'd have to have rules, right, O-Man?"

Owen's smile stretched so wide, I could count how many teeth were in his little mouth. "I didn't hear Mom make any rules."

"You two…" She wagged her finger at us. "That was low."

Owen and I couldn't catch up to Beth after she took off, so we devised a plan. A risky one. We stopped our ATV and Owen hopped off and pretended he was sick. The kid could be an actor the way he clutched at his stomach and moaned when she circled back to check if we were okay. When she got off and walked over to us, Owen hopped back in the ATV and grabbed on tight while I hit the gas. We literally smoked her—left her coughing in a cloud of dust in our wake.

I raised my hand to Owen for a high five. "What I tell ya? Girls go to Jupiter…."

Owen smacked my hand hard. "To get more stupider."

"I am not eating a bug, you cheaters!" Beth said.

I chuckled. "That's right. You're not. You're eating *three,* remember?"

⸻

Owen fell asleep almost as soon as we got in the car to head back to Scottsdale. We'd spent a few hours touring the Red Rocks, and then hiked the Cathedral Rock Trail for the most gorgeous view. I could have taken a nap myself if I didn't have a two-hour drive ahead of me.

"Thanks for today. I can't remember the last time Owen and I had this much fun."

"Thank *you.* You let me monopolize your entire day."

Beth glanced over her shoulder into the back seat and lowered her voice. "He really took a liking to you. He's been having trouble connecting to men since Tom and I split up. Unfortunately, the year before we called it quits wasn't pretty. There was a lot of yelling, and Tom has a really deep voice so it used to scare Owen."

I glanced at her and back to the road. "I'm sorry that you both went through that. But he's a great kid. I would've never thought he had trouble connecting to anyone. He was so outgoing."

She smiled. "Everyone is outgoing around you."

That was the furthest thing from the truth these days. "Tell that to my staff. I hear most of them are a little afraid of me."

She laughed. "Why would they be afraid of you?"

"Sometimes I'm a little…cranky, I guess."

"Well, you must've left that side of you back in New York, because Cranky Pants wasn't here today."

I arched a brow. "Cranky Pants?"

"Sorry. I teach third grade and have a six-year-old. My lingo is somewhere under the age of ten most days. I can't remember the last time I actually hung out with adults, outside of my coworkers and family."

"How come?"

"Most of my friends are married, and I haven't wanted to go out with my few single friends yet. They're sort of on the prowl all the time, and I'm not ready to get back out there."

I nodded. It made me wonder, if things ended between me and Gia, how the hell would I get back out there? The thought of being with another woman seemed more torture than tantalizing, and I didn't even want to think about *Gia* getting back out there. "Yeah. That must be hard."

"You know what's sad, I miss having a man around the house to make repairs more than I miss the intimate time. Maybe I'll join one of those dating websites and when it asks what I'm looking for in a man, I'll post my repair list. How do you think that will go over? Single, twenty-nine-year-old mother of adorable, six-year-old boy, seeks man with carpentry, electrical, and plumbing skills." She laughed. "Think I'll get any responses?"

I looked over at her. "Wear the right outfit with a little cleavage and you'll get men who respond even if you write you're looking for someone to castrate."

She shook her head. "Sad…but true."

We talked the entire drive home, most of the time reminiscing about all the funny memories we had of her dad. Being here, talking about him, really made me realize how short life was. And how I'd let the stupid shit make me forget someone who was important to me. When we pulled to the curb, I parked.

"Listen, Beth. I'm really sorry I lost touch with your dad, and that you and I only text a few times a year. He was really important in my life, and I didn't show him that the last ten years."

She smiled sadly. "Just because you didn't talk to him all the time doesn't mean he didn't know you cared about him. He knew. I know he did."

It dawned on me that Beth was making me feel better, when it should be the other way around. "Sorry. I shouldn't be unloading my guilty conscience on you. I should be the one listening. Making you feel better."

"Don't be silly. You made me feel better all day. I needed to be able to talk about the good times with Dad with someone. Mom is still too raw, and I feel better right now than I have for days. I'd been focusing on the loss, instead of the life I had with him. And you made me remember that I have a lot to be thankful for."

"Well, I don't know how I did that. But I'm glad to hear you're at least feeling better."

"Why don't you come in? I'll make us a quick dinner, pasta or something."

"I'm actually kind of wiped. Before we started to drive, I thought about asking you to drive and hopping in the back to let my tongue hang out while I slept, like Owen."

Beth looked over at her son. "He does sort of sleep like a puppy, doesn't he?"

I chuckled. "You said it, not me."

"Well, thank you again for today. Are you up for something tomorrow?"

"You bet. I'll bring lunch. PB and J for me and my little buddy, and I'll bring a knife and fork for your three Arizona fat bugs."

"I'm not eating bugs, cheater."

She opened her car door. I looked back when the interior light illuminated, and Owen hadn't budged. "He's really out, huh?"

"The kid can sleep through the high-pitched wail of a smoke alarm inside his room."

"Not sure that's a good thing. Are you going to try and wake him?"

"No. I'll just carry him in and put him to bed."

"I'll do it." Owen was a pretty big kid for his age. He had to weigh fifty or sixty pounds. "He's at least half your body weight."

Beth wasn't kidding. Owen didn't even flutter his eyes open as I unbuckled him from the back, lifted him out of the car, and set him over my shoulder fireman-style. He was totally dead weight to carry, too.

"Where's his room?" I asked once we were inside the kitchen.

"Down the hall, first door on the left. I need to run to the bathroom."

"Okay."

Owen's room was dark, and I didn't want to risk tripping over something, so I flipped on the light. As I suspected, he didn't mind in the slightest. I gently set him down on his bed and pulled the covers over him. I'd never tucked a kid in before at night, and the moment caught me off guard. I studied Owen's little face for a minute. He was such a great kid, so full of adventure and happiness.

What would it be like to tuck my own son in every night?

I'd read him a story. He'd definitely like scary books. No pansy-ass stories for my kid about trains that talked. I smiled thinking of Gia coming in while I was reading something totally age-inappropriate and scolding us for the tenth time. I'd watch him sleep for a few minutes, before shutting the lights off and heading to my own room. Where I'd proceed to do dirty shit to his mother.

As fast as the warm feeling had come over me as I imagined that play out in my head, I suddenly remembered I wouldn't be tucking my own son in every night. I'd be tucking *Elliott's* son in.

I took one last look at Owen and headed for his door.

Beth was in the kitchen pouring wine. She had two glasses on the table.

"Would you like a glass of wine?"

"Nah. I'm good. But thanks. I'll see you tomorrow? How about around eleven?"

Her smile fell, but she forced the edges back up. "Sure. That sounds great. Thanks again for today, Heath."

Back in my hotel room, I cracked open a beer from the mini bar and debated over texting Gia. I'd told her I needed some time, which I did, so it really wasn't fair to her to keep making contact until I was sure where I stood with things. I'd been checking in with Oak twice a day, having him tell me she looked fine and things were good. But it wasn't enough. I needed to hear her, even if it was just words in a text. Yet I still settled on Oak.

Rush: How's everything going?

Oak: Everything's smooth here, boss.

Rush: How's Gia? Does she look okay? Is anyone bothering her?

After I typed it, I pictured a big gloating smile on Oak's face. I didn't give a fuck. I needed to know.

Oak: Your woman looks good. Came in on time, and I'm paying extra attention to her.

Rush: Is she sitting enough?

A few seconds later, I got a response. Only it wasn't from Oak.

Gia: Are you texting with Oak right now?
Shit.

Rush: Yeah. Just checking in.

Gia: That's funny. Because he just looked up at me, then texted into his phone.

I smiled. It felt good to hear her words. I'd missed her calling me on my bullshit.

Rush: I might've asked how you were doing...he wasn't supposed to let you know.

Gia: The man is six-foot-six, inconspicuous is out.

I laughed.

Rush: I'll try to remember that.

She went quiet after that. I couldn't let things end that way.

Rush: So now that I'm caught anyway. How are you feeling?

A new message from Oak popped up.

Oak: She's sitting right now, looking down and smiling. She's good, boss.

I hadn't even noticed how tense my shoulders were, until they relaxed hearing that.

Gia: I'm feeling good. No more spotting or anything at all. But I think I grew two inches around my waist overnight. I had to sneak into your office an hour ago and loop a rubber band through the buttonhole of my pants and onto the button. They were so tight.

A vision of Gia with a big round belly popped into my head. I closed my eyes to block everything else out and nab a better look. God, I loved her pregnant. It made me want to go back home just to see her belly again. And then…it fucking hit me.

Elliott's baby is in that belly.

It was like my brain wanted to torture me. I'd feel like everything was fine, somehow forgetting the shit storm of late, and then it would thrust back into my memory with a vengeance. Those thirty seconds where I forgot felt so good, but it only made it worse when the truth slapped me in the face once again—like cutting open a raw wound over and over.

Rush: Glad you're feeling well. Have a good night, Gia.

CHAPTER 9

Rush

All hell had broken lose.

I'd shown up to pick up Beth and Owen at eleven the next day, just like we'd agreed upon. But when I got there, the two of them definitely weren't ready to go sightseeing. In fact, it looked like they'd both lost their sanity a little. I was tempted to stay in the doorway for a while to watch the comedy show going on, but that would've just led to further damage. Water was spraying full blast from the kitchen faucet, and the two of them were standing in ankle-deep water. Owen had a cracked bucket and was scooping up water from the floor and dumping it into an outdoor garbage can. Only the crack in his bucket leaked out half the contents before he lifted it from the floor to the top of the garbage can. Beth had two hands wrapped around the faucet handle attempting to stop the water, yet it continued to spray all over the place—including directly into her face. She looked like she'd been standing there for a while. Not to mention, a kitchen cabinet hung broken from its hinges, and was that... *Cheerios* floating in the water?

"What the heck is going on here?"

Beth answered frantically, screaming over the loud sound of the water spray. "Thank God you're here! How do you shut off the water?"

"Turn the handle under the sink?"

She opened her clenched fist to reveal a rusted valve knob. "It broke off!"

"Where's your main?"

"My what?"

"Forget it." I turned around and jogged back outside. Circling the perimeter of her property, I found the main and twisted off all the water coming into her house. When I returned to chaos central, the water had stopped, and the two of them were catching their breath.

"What happened?"

"At night, we put the kitchen garbage can in the sink to keep it away from Mark."

"Mark?"

Owen responded with a shrug. "Our cat. She's a girl."

"Mark likes to knock over the garbage to eat it," Beth said. "So we put it out of her reach. She must've jumped up on the kitchen counter and knocked the garbage over and somehow turned on the water in the process. When I got up this morning, the kitchen was already flooded. I tried to turn it off, but the stupid knob broke off in my hand."

I took off my shoes and started to roll up my pants. "Why didn't you call me?"

She pointed to the corner next to the refrigerator where something was floating. "I tried. I dropped my phone. I don't have your number memorized."

Wading into the kitchen, I took the bucket from Owen's hands. "Got a shop vac, buddy?"

"In the basement."

"Come on. Show me."

I followed Owen into the basement and grabbed the vacuum. Owen was looking down with both hands in his pocket. His pants and shirt were soaked, and he looked defeated.

I set the vacuum back down and knelt. "Everything's going to be okay. We'll clean it up."

He spoke with his head still hanging. "My dad said I was supposed to take care of the house and Mom. But I didn't know how to fix it."

Crap.

I nudged his chin up. "I think what he meant was, he wants you to help out whenever you can. And you did that. From what I saw, you were scooping buckets as fast as the water poured in. Without you, the water would probably be to at least your waist, instead of your ankles."

His eyes widened. "Really?"

I lied. "Yep. You pretty much saved the house, and you stayed pretty calm from what I saw. That's the number one thing you need to do in an emergency, you know. Stay calm."

His frown turned up to a grin. "Mom was freaking out. She wasn't calm, was she?"

I smiled. "Nope. So it's a good thing she had you. But I'll teach you some things so that if this type of thing ever happens again, you'll be even more ready for it."

"Okay!"

I carried the shop vac upstairs and put it in the kitchen. Beth was in her room getting changed, so I used the opportunity to give Owen a lesson. "Come on, let me take you outside where the water main is."

The two of us went outside, and I showed him where to turn off the water coming into the house. Then I took him back to the kitchen and gave him an electricity-meets-water lesson. God forbid the water would have been any higher, it could've come up to the electrical outlets and electrified the water they were standing in.

Beth emerged towel drying her hair and wearing dry clothes. "Owen, go get changed into something warm."

"But I'm going to help Heath fix the kitchen."

"You are, are you? Okay…well…go put on a bathing suit and take off the wet shirt and socks, at least."

"Okay, Mom!" He took off running toward his room.

"I'm sorry about this," Beth said. "I've ruined our sightseeing morning."

"Don't be silly. I made a list of shit I wanted to do out here; first was to see the Red Rocks and second was to clean up a flood."

She laughed. "Thanks for being a good sport. But you don't have to help me clean it up. I'll do it."

"I got it. Go sit down for a few minutes. You look sort of a wreck."

"Gee, thanks."

While I vacuumed up all the water, Owen did as I'd instructed him to—drying off his mom's cell phone and putting it inside a baggie full of rice. Beth came back into the kitchen with a stack of towels when the excess water from the floor was gone. She started to lay them on the floor and dry the rest of the area.

"What happened to that cabinet door?"

"Don't ask," she said. "We ran around like two chickens without our heads until you got here. I dropped my cell. Owen tried to grab the Cheerios from the cabinet while he scooped water because he got hungry, and he wound up dumping the entire box into the water. And then I asked him to get me the electrical tape so I could try and tape up the spray. He couldn't reach it, so he used the cabinet door as a stool and broke it."

I chuckled. "You had a pretty bad morning."

For the next three hours, my shadow and I went about fixing things. After everything dried, we went to the plumbing store and picked up the parts I needed to install a new faucet and valve handle. Owen stuck next to me the entire time. It was really freaking cute.

"First, I'm going to fix the valve handle that broke off. That way when we install the new faucet, we can turn the main back on and control things from under here in case anything goes wrong."

"Got it." He nodded.

The wood in the cabinet underneath the sink was soaked even though there wasn't any visible water anymore. It would probably take a few days to dry out. I slipped off my shirt before sitting down on the floor. I'd need to be on my back inside the cabinet to work on the broken pipe stem and handle. I had to swallow my laughter when little man yanked off his shirt, too. Owen managed to fit inside the kitchen cabinet and watch everything I did while I repaired the valve stem and handle. And he asked some pretty damn good questions while we worked.

"Did it break because it was rusty?"

"Yeah, that's what happens. The rust causes the metal to disintegrate and then it falls apart when you need to touch it one day. Basically, the rotten metal crumbles."

"So should I change the ones in the two bathrooms? I looked under the sinks before. I think they're getting rusty, too."

What a kid…wasn't even asking me to do it. Figured he'd take it on himself after he watched me do one. He took the responsibility of looking after his mother pretty seriously. I was familiar with that and respected the hell out of it.

"That's a good thought. I'll check 'em out and see if maybe we should do that together."

A little while later, his mind had obviously wandered. "Dad would've been cursing a lot if he was here."

"Yeah? Well, between us, I curse sometimes, too." Translation—a fuck of a lot.

"He gets mad a lot. That's why he doesn't like it here anymore."

I stopped tightening the bolt and looked over at Owen. "All adults get mad from time to time. I'm sure your dad liked it here. It's just that sometimes people need to be separate to like each other again."

"Do you live separate from your wife?"

No, but I just ran two-thousand miles to get away from the woman I love.

"I don't have a wife, buddy."

"How come?"

"I just don't. Sometimes it takes people a while to find the right person and know it's time to get married." *I'm having this conversation with a six-year-old. While under a sink. Both of us shirtless.*

"I'm never getting married."

I chuckled. "That's what I always said, too. But that might change when you meet the right person."

After we finished changing the hardware under the sink, the two of us climbed out. Beth was standing in the kitchen and handed us each a towel.

I dried my hands and looked over at Owen. "Thanks for the help, O-Man."

When my eyes returned to Beth, I noticed hers were not looking at her son like mine were. Hers were focused on my chest. It took a good thirty seconds for her to raise her eyes to meet mine. And then I saw her face.

Shit.

It was an expression I knew well. Mostly because I wore it every time Gia was around. I might've been full of myself, but I was pretty sure I knew the *I want to lick your body* face when I saw it. Normally, it was my favorite face on a woman when I was undressed. But not today. Not with this woman. I grabbed my shirt from the kitchen counter and slipped it back on, attempting to break the heavy feeling I suddenly felt.

"Owen here showed me how to fix the sink. Kid's pretty smart. Must take after his dad." I winked.

"Yeah. Mom can't even fix the remote when the back falls off." The kid had a great sense of humor for only six.

"Two wise guys. Just what I needed after the morning I've had," Beth said. "What do you say, you go wash up, Owen, and we'll go grab some lunch."

"Okay. I'm really hungry!"

Owen took off and left the two of us alone in the kitchen.

Beth tilted her head. "You have a lot more tattoos than you did when I moved out here from New York."

"Yeah. I've slowed down now. But there's still a few more I'd like to get before my skin starts seeing its sagging days."

"Trust me, you have a long way to go before that body sees any sag." She looked down and then up at me. "You look good, Heath. Really good."

And there went that feeling again. Like I was doing something wrong for her even saying that. It nagged at me, but I didn't want to be rude. "Thanks. You look good, too."

Luckily, Owen ran back to the kitchen. I was pretty sure he only had a chance to wash one hand, but he'd live eating dirty. "Mom's paying...so what do you feel like? Caviar? Kobe beef?"

Owen wrinkled up his nose. "How about Taco Bell?"

"You got it, buddy."

———

After lunch, where Owen told me one bad joke after another, we went back to their house so I could finish up fixing the faucet. It turned out to be a bigger project than I anticipated, and I wound up going back to the plumbing store a few more times before everything was back in working order. My little buddy stuck to me like glue again.

Beth had been running some errands and came back with two sacks full of groceries. I walked to the door to grab them from her, and when I turned around, Owen had his hands in the air to give him one.

"Owen, I spoke to Jack's Mom. He wants to know if you want to come over for a little while to play Xbox. He just got some new game."

His eyes lit up, and then he looked at me. "Are we done?"

"Sure are. Why don't you go have fun? You did a lot of work today."

Ten minutes later there was a honk out front and Owen took off. He made it halfway down the driveway before he ran back to me. "Will you be here when I get home?"

"Probably not. But you go have fun. You earned it after all you did today."

I didn't expect it, but the little guy wrapped his arms around my waist. "Thanks for helping us today."

I bent down so I could look him in the eye. "It was my pleasure. And, Owen, you're doing a great job taking care of Mom and the house."

"Thanks."

After Beth came back in from talking to Owen's friend's mom, she grabbed two beers out of the refrigerator and handed me one.

She tilted her head toward the living room. "Come on. Let's go sit."

Together we sat on the couch. "Do you remember when Dad caught us fooling around in the living room on our old blue couch?"

To this day, I felt bad about that. "Of course. He took off his work boot and chucked it at me when I ran for the door. Thing had a steel toe. Hurt like a bitch. But I deserved it." I sucked down half of my beer.

"You know, that week we had together means a lot to me."

Beth had been a virgin when I ruined our friendship by taking things where I led them.

"It meant a lot to me, too. And I'm sorry about the way I ended things. I was...a prick."

She smiled. "You weren't really. We'd agreed that it was just fooling around, nothing more. But I didn't know how to separate sex from emotions back then."

That was one thing I had always been good at. Sex was just sex. The only emotions I associated with sex were excitement and eagerness. Until out of nowhere, a certain little sassy thing showed up one night behind my bar.

"We were young. You grew up a lot faster than I did."

"I grew up *too* fast. Married at twenty-two, a baby at twenty-three. Both of those led to divorce at twenty-eight. Tom wasn't a bad guy. It was just that neither of us had lived much before we got together at twenty. We hadn't experienced much."

"You got a great kid out of it, at least. Owen's great."

"You were great with him. He really took to you. Do you want kids someday?"

I traced my finger along the top of the beer bottle. "I didn't think I did. But…it's complicated."

She smiled. "That's what you said when I asked you if you were seeing anyone."

I felt like I should open up a little bit. "She's…having a kid. It's just not mine. Happened before we met."

"Oh. Wow. Well…that definitely makes it complicated. But I hope you don't let that stop you from being with her. Because that wouldn't bode well for the outlook of my future either—being a single mom of a six-year-old and all."

I nodded. "It's complicated."

"So you've said…"

I started to think out loud. "I just don't know if I can be a dad to someone else's kid. Especially not the guy whose kid she's having."

"I watched you today with Owen. Trust me, you're a natural. And if you're worried about DNA, don't be. Was my father like a dad to you?"

"Yeah. He was."

"You didn't share blood."

"I guess."

"Was your biological father like a dad to you?"

My face answered without the necessity of words. Beth had been there for the years of shit with my sperm donor.

"See. And you *did* share blood. A father has nothing to do with DNA."

Deep down, I knew she was right. But she didn't understand my fucked-up situation.

"It's..." I went to say complicated, and then realized I sounded like a broken record. "Hard. It's hard."

"Everything happens for a reason, Heath. You're here to remember my dad. I don't think you're supposed to use this time to mourn him. I think my dad's death is meant to be a reminder to you that you can be a parent without the biology."

I took a minute and really gave it some thought. Maybe she was right. As strange as it sounds, I think her dad would want his death to teach me something. That was just the kind of man he was. A good one. A real father figure.

Looking up, I found Beth watching me. I squinted. "When did you become such a crack psychologist?"

"You want the truth?"

"Of course."

"Today when you got here, my white shirt was soaked, and I didn't even have a bra on. My nipples were greeting you, and you didn't even notice. Earlier, when you had no shirt on, I practically salivated at the sight of your six-pack. *It's been a while.* You looked like you were ready to run for the hills when you caught me staring. So I figured out pretty quickly that whatever was complicated—meant complicated love. And even though a part of me is sort of jealous, I've never wanted anything but happiness for you. Neither did my dad. So it feels right that maybe he—and I—can help you see things clearly."

I stared at her. Shaking my head, I said. "You haven't changed a bit. Still as good a friend at twenty-nine as you were at nine."

Beth leaned forward and took my hand. "Let's enjoy each other and the memory of my dad this week. Like the old days, like brother and sister. If my mind happens to wander to your six-pack or ass, just ignore it...it's hormones."

I arched a brow. "My ass? I thought you were only checking out my abs?"

She smiled. "Only when you're facing forward."

CHAPTER 10

Gia

"**O**mmmmm."

Sitting in lotus position, with my palms together, I tried my best to follow along to the pregnancy meditation video I was watching on YouTube.

A very pregnant woman was demonstrating moves being narrated by a man who had a soothing British accent. A pretty beach was the backdrop. I'd never tried anything like this before, but if there was ever a time in my life to attempt it, it was now.

"Breathe in and breathe out," he said. "Imagine that your baby can hear all of the positive thoughts emanating from your mind. Send love to the baby through your loins."

My loins?

Gosh, I hoped my baby couldn't hear any of the negative thoughts going through my mind lately. That would have been detrimental.

I'd decided to try yoga and meditation as a way to relax, get my mind off all of the stress I'd been experiencing lately, but I wasn't quite sure if this was working for me.

The tune playing in the background of the video sounded like a cross between a lullaby and instrumental Chinese meditation music.

Some of the things that came out of the narrator's mouth made me crack up. "Send peaceful vibes to your infant... imagine a beautiful light flowing up into your vagina and traveling to the baby."

Into my what?

For some reason, all I could think about was what I imagined Rush would be saying if he were here. He would totally be making fun of this.

"I'll travel through your vagina, alright. Like a fuckin' rocket."

"Let your love flow into the baby as you position yourself into downward dog."

There was Rush again: *"I've got lots of love to give you—doggy-style."*

I just kept hearing Rush and laughing, and that made me totally unable to concentrate on what I was supposed to be doing.

Well, of course, I was hearing the old Rush, the one who wasn't broken by the horrible twist of fate we'd encountered, the one who still talked to me.

Maybe I couldn't get Rush out of my mind because I had no idea where he was or what he was doing. He'd check in on me through Oak but still hadn't told me what he was up to or when he was coming back. In the meantime, I had no choice but to just continue on with my life, trying to write during the day and then working my shifts at The Heights at night. The only good thing was that my writing was really taking off. Not sure if that was because mental anguish spawned creativity or what. But I was seriously kicking ass with my story, and that was literally the only consolation about this entire ordeal.

"Embrace your child and imagine running through a field toward it."

For some reason, when the man said that, all I could picture was running through an open field with my baby and Rush by my side. I just couldn't imagine going through this journey without him, couldn't foresee life without him. Whenever I imagined anything pertaining to the baby, Rush was always there. That was going to be a hard habit to break.

———

That evening at work, I wasn't feeling any more relaxed despite my best attempts earlier in the day. I'd stare down the hallway toward Rush's office as if he was in there. His presence was everywhere, especially here. Being at The Heights was always the hardest part of the day to get through. Rush's stamp was all over this place.

Oak made a point to come up to me during a slow period. "Hey, Gia. How are you feeling tonight?"

I shrugged. "I'm okay."

God, that was such a lie.

"You sure about that? You seem really down. But I get it."

"I miss Rush," I confessed. "Has he checked in with you?"

Oak flashed a sympathetic smile. "Not today." He paused. "But I think he was heading to the Grand Canyon, right?"

"The Grand Canyon? He's out west?"

Oak's face dropped. "*Shit*. You didn't know he was out in Arizona?"

"No. I had no idea. What is Rush doing in Arizona?"

"Me and my big mouth." He shook his head. "I shouldn't have said anything, but I didn't think it was a secret. He went to a funeral out there. A man he was friendly with when he was younger died. Name was Pat."

My heart was beating out of my chest. "Oh my God. The guy who was like a father to him growing up."

Oak nodded. "It was sudden. A heart attack."

My heart broke for him. For that to have happened in the midst of everything else seemed so unfair. Then my heartbeat really started to accelerate because I remembered the whole story he told me about Pat...and his daughter. *Beth*. I definitely always remembered her name. The one he'd slept with. Pat was her father. They were good friends before they ended up sleeping together. So, if he was in Arizona...he was with Beth.

My roommates had accumulated a lot of stuff over the summer that they couldn't bring back with them or that they couldn't store in the City, stuff like boogie boards and surfing gear. So the following day I organized a rummage sale for those items in the house that they couldn't take with them.

They agreed to let me keep a percentage of the profits in exchange for standing outside all day hawking the stuff. I needed money now that I'd be moving home and would soon be unemployed.

Earlier in the week, I'd hung up fliers around town advertising the sale. I added a lot of my own personal belongings to the mix. I had more shoes and clothes than I knew what to do with, and now that the baby was coming, I needed to downsize. So I rounded up a bunch of stuff I wanted to add to the pot. The less I had to take back to the City with me, the better.

Putting two outdoor tables together side by side, I laid all of the items out. Some of the bigger things, like surfboards, I propped up behind my chair.

Volume was slow. Cars that happened to drive by would stop, but the majority of the time the people wouldn't buy anything. Every ten minutes or so, someone who'd seen one of the fliers would walk over.

A little after lunch, a flurry of people showed up all at once. I sold off all of the larger surf items to one buyer, and I was left with about half of the other things. The small crowd also left behind a mess on the table of the items they'd rifled through that I needed to clean up.

My back was turned away from the street as I reorganized the clothes and small goods on display.

"What's all this?"

His voice vibrated through me.

I turned around so suddenly that it made me a little dizzy.

My heart nearly stopped at the sight of him. Rush had never looked so amazing. Maybe it was the absence, maybe it was the pregnancy hormones, but it took everything in me not to leap into his arms. The recognition of his scent was both beautiful and painful all at once. I longed for him but wouldn't allow myself to move toward him.

Feeling off balance, I muttered, "Rush…"

"Hi, Gia."

The Rush who'd left a couple of weeks ago was a total wreck. The Rush standing before me no longer had red eyes and a pained expression. I wouldn't say he looked happy, but he looked at peace, like the time away had somehow changed something in him. What exactly that meant for me, I was still trying to figure out.

Blowing out a shaky breath, I said, "You're back."

"I am."

My eyes were working overtime, scrolling up, down, and across him for any signs that he'd been with someone else, that he'd fallen for another woman, or that his heart was no longer mine—as if you could tell those things by just looking.

He was wearing a jacket I'd never seen before. I wondered if he bought it in Arizona. His hair was no longer mussed from running his fingers through it. He didn't smell like cigarettes, either, so I was happy to know that he probably hadn't fallen off the wagon on his travels out west.

"I'm so sorry to hear about Pat."

He squinted like he was trying to figure out how I knew. "Yeah. It was unexpected."

"Oak told me that's where you've been."

"He did, did he?"

"I know you didn't want me to know where you were. He accidentally let it slip."

God, I couldn't stop staring at him. I wanted nothing more than for him to touch me, hold me, kiss me…anything. I couldn't recall my physical need for him ever being as strong as it was in this moment. I would have been completely fine with forgetting about things for a night and just going inside my place and taking all of our frustrations out on each other. But of course, that was fantasy; the hard stare aimed at me right now was reality.

"It wasn't that I didn't want you to know. Where I was in relation to me and you is irrelevant. I needed to get away, get into a different headspace that wasn't based on anger. And I needed to do that apart from you. Unfortunately, Pat died in the midst of it, and my being away became mostly about mourning him and only partly about clearing my head."

I continued staring at him, my body profoundly aware of his presence, yearning for him to touch me.

"Are you okay?" I asked.

"Yeah, I am. His death definitely knocked the wind out of me, though." He looked down at my stomach, then back up at me. "Are you alright?"

I shrugged. "Hanging in there."

He looked at all of the items still strewn on the table. "Why are you selling this stuff?"

"It's almost the end of the summer, and we've all accumulated a lot of junk. Plus, I needed to downsize."

Rush sucked in his cheeks. "Downsize? Sounds like I wasn't the only one who did a lot of thinking while I was gone."

I looked down and nodded. "I've decided to move back to Queens."

"And your mind's made up…just like that? No discussion?"

"I need to do what's best for us." My hand automatically went to my belly. I'd been doing that a lot lately—rubbing and not even realizing I was doing it.

"And that's running away? Because fucking running away solves everything, right?" he said bitterly.

"I'm not running away. I'm just doing what I feel I need to at this point in time."

We stared at each other. After a long time, I took a deep breath and said, "Can you tell me you want to be with me?

That you can accept the hand we've been dealt and move on?"

His face had been hard, revealing his anger at hearing about me downsizing in anticipation of my move back. But when I asked that question, his features softened. That told me his answer: he felt bad that he couldn't bring himself to tell me to stay with him. The trip might've done him some personal good, but apparently the internal debate he'd been having didn't come out in my favor.

Rush looked down. "I wish I could, Gia. I wish I could."

CHAPTER 11

Gia

I sat out front with the unsold goods until long after dark. When Rush left hours ago, I took a seat in a beach chair that I should've been trying to sell and didn't get back out of it. If someone had a question, I answered from the chair, not even bothering to get up. If they wanted to pay, they had to bring me the cash. His short visit had drained all of my energy.

It took everything in me to force myself to get up and pack everything that hadn't sold. Most of the stuff I just tossed into boxes, figuring tomorrow I'd sort out which of my roommates had given it to me to sell. I folded the tables and dragged the bigger stuff into the garage.

I wanted nothing more than to plop down on my bed, but I'd been sitting in the sun outside all day, and then dragged the boxes in while it was humid tonight, so I was pretty sure that I could use a shower.

In the bathroom while I undressed, I noticed a little spotting in my underwear. That had happened to me before, and my doctor had said as long as it was light, it wasn't that unusual. So I tried not to get alarmed, even though it sort of freaked me out. But after I washed my hair, I looked down and noticed that the water running down my leg had a pinkish tint to it.

Scared, I rinsed off and grabbed my cell phone, calling the doctor while dripping in the shower stall. It was late, so an answering service picked up and said that the doctor would call me back. By the time I dried off and wrapped myself in a towel, my cell was already ringing.

"Hi, Dr. Daniels. Thank you for calling back so quickly."

"What's going on, Gia? The service said you're having some bleeding? Is there any cramping with it?"

"No. No cramping. I had a little spotting and then when I went in the shower, I noticed the color of the water coming down my leg was pink."

"Did you do anything out of the ordinary today in terms of exertion? Any heavy lifting or anything?

"I moved some boxes around…but I didn't really do that much lifting. I mostly just dragged things." *God, I hope my stupid tag sale didn't hurt the baby.*

"Okay. Well, one drop of blood can turn a good amount of water pink. And a small amount of spotting is somewhat common, especially early on. So don't get yourself too frantic over it. But we should probably bring you in to get checked out. My office is closed, so why don't you meet me over at South Hampton Hospital in about an hour? Go to the Emergency Room, and just tell the nurse that you're meeting me. She'll set you up with an outpatient admission and check your vitals if you get there before I do."

"Okay, Dr. Daniels. Thank you. I'll see you soon."

As soon as I hung up, I raced around like a lunatic to get dressed, even though the hospital was only a ten-minute drive. He'd said not to panic, but that was as good as telling an ice cube not to melt in the sun.

After I was dressed, I picked up my cell to call Rush. My finger hovered over his name in my contacts, and then I remembered Rush and I...we weren't...whatever we were anymore. I needed to do this alone. But I was also afraid to drive, in the off chance that the bleeding became heavier. So instead, I dialed Riley.

"Hey. Where are you?"

"I'm on my way home from a beach volleyball tournament. About three blocks away from the house. Why? What's up? Do you need something? Some ice cream and pickles, maybe?" she teased.

"No. I need a ride to the Emergency Room."

———

"Everything seems fine." Dr. Daniels snapped off his rubber gloves and stood at the end of the exam table.

I took my feet out of the stirrups and sat up. "So the bleeding is normal, then?"

"The normal production of hormones when you're pregnant can sometimes cause changes to your cervix, making it softer, and on occasion more prone to bleeding. You're actually still spotting a little, so I'm inclined to say that's all it is. If it were a larger amount of blood, I'd be more concerned. Your sonogram looks okay, but I'm troubled by your blood pressure. It's a little on the high side tonight."

"I'm really nervous...and...I had some stress today."

"I'm sure that's all it is. I bet it comes down naturally within a few hours. But because it's a little high and you've had some spotting, I'm going to admit you overnight for monitoring. Just as a precaution. The chances of a miscarriage are slim, but it's best you stay since you're already here."

I was glad he didn't check my blood pressure again because the moment he mentioned miscarriage and admitting me, my heart started to race. No doubt my blood pressure would be speeding up to match.

Dr. Daniels went to talk to the nurse and sent Riley in to visit.

"Are you okay? The doctor said you're staying."

"Yeah. He said it's just a precaution."

She searched my face and took my hand. "You look nervous."

I forced a smile. "I am. I feel so helpless. And I'm so mad at myself for doing that tag sale today."

Her eyes widened. "He said the tag sale caused this?"

"No. But he asked if I'd lifted any boxes. I hadn't really lifted any heavy ones, because I know I'm not supposed to. But I did shuffle things around a lot."

"God. I shouldn't have gone to volleyball. I should've stayed and helped you."

"Don't be silly. This isn't your fault. The doctor doesn't even think it's mine. I just…I could've been more careful."

Riley stuck around and kept me company for hours. At about ten-thirty, they finally moved me from the Emergency Room to a regular room upstairs. It had two beds, but luckily the one next to me was empty so I had the room to myself. My eyelids were so heavy that I started to doze while Riley was talking to me.

"I guess I'm boring you." She laughed when my eyes fluttered back open.

"No. I'm sorry. I'm just so tired."

"It's late. And it's been a long day. First, you were in the sun for the tag sale, and then this. I might take that bed next to you soon."

I smiled. "You should go home."

"You sure? What if you need something?"

I lifted the little buzzer the nurse had clipped to the railing on my bed. "I have a bell. I'll call the nurse."

"Okay. But call me if you need anything." She leaned over and hugged me. "I'll be back first thing in the morning, G. Get some sleep."

That was the last thing I remembered before I stirred sometime in the middle of the night. When my eyes came into focus in the dark, I was confused where I was at first. But even more confused to find Rush slouched in the chair next to my bed, sound asleep. I hadn't called him? Had I?

I sat up in an attempt to clear my head. The soft rustling of the sheets moving must have been enough to wake him

"Hey," he whispered. "How are you feeling?"

"Okay. But...how did you know I was here?"

"Birdbrain called into work sick earlier."

"Birdbrain?"

"Your buddy, Riley. She called in saying she wasn't feeling well and needed to stay home. She sounded fine to me. But when I asked her how you were...she acted funny. I tried your cell to see if everything was okay, and you weren't answering."

"My phone died in the Emergency Room, and I didn't have a charger."

"I got worried and went to the house. Birdbrain wouldn't let me in. She said you were fine and sleeping. Something was off, so I fired her ass and told her she wouldn't qualify for the full summer season bonus that she was so close to getting."

"You fired her?"

He shrugged. "Got her to give up where you were."

I closed my eyes. "Sorry I made you worry."

"Why didn't you call me?"

I looked away. "I need to start doing things on my own. Whether I'm happy, sad, mad, or scared, my first instinct is to pick up the phone and call you."

Rush stayed quiet for so long that I had to look and see what he was doing. His head was in his hands. "I really fucked things up between us."

"No, you didn't. Everything that happened is my fault."

Rush stood. "Scoot over."

I moved to one side while Rush pulled the curtain around us, even though no one else was in the room. Then he slipped off his shoes and climbed into bed. He lay on his back and tucked me into the crux of his arm and began to stroke my hair.

"I was so scared. I think I broke a hundred miles an hour driving here."

"I was scared, too. That's probably why my blood pressure was high, and the doctor wanted to keep me overnight."

"I'm sorry I wasn't here for you."

"Well, you didn't have any way of knowing."

"Doesn't matter."

Rush stroked my hair, and we were both silent for a long time. It felt so good to be in bed with him, even if it was just snuggling. The warmth of his body, the way I folded and fit so perfectly in his arms, everything felt right again even in the midst of a crazy twenty-four hours.

"The doctor mentioned miscarriage last night," I said. "Even though I'm not even halfway done with this pregnancy, and my life would probably be so much easier if I wasn't…" I couldn't even say it out loud. "I mean…it would fix so many broken things. But I don't want to lose this baby, Rush. I already love him, and the thought of anything happening terrifies me."

Rush kissed the top of my head and squeezed me closer. "Yeah."

"I'm sorry. I'm so, so sorry that everything turned out the way it did. I'd give anything for you to be this baby's father."

Rush went quiet again. His voice cracked when he finally spoke. "Me, too, Gia. Me, too."

Getting that off my chest and being held in his arms made me feel so relaxed that soon I started to drift off to sleep again. Rush's groggy voice interrupted my slumber. "Him."

"Hmmm?"

"You said *him*. You think our little guy is a boy, too."

———

I woke to a beam of sunshine warming my face. Squinting, I looked over at the empty space next to me on the bed, and a sudden panic came over me. *Where's Rush?*

I calmed slightly when I found someone sitting in the chair. Only…it wasn't Rush. Trying to hide my disappointment, I forced a smile as best I could. "Hi, Dad. When did you get here? And where's Rush?"

He leaned forward to the edge of his seat and pushed back the hair from my forehead. "I've been here about ten minutes. Haven't seen Rush. But I'm glad *he* called me early this morning. Why the hell didn't you call me, Gia?"

I sighed. "I'm sorry. I didn't want to worry you. It was late by the time they admitted me to a room."

"You should've called me the minute you thought something was wrong. I would have called the local precinct and sent someone to pick you up and take you to the ER, lights and sirens."

I smiled. "That's exactly why I didn't call you. I'm fine. I spoke to the doctor on the phone, and he had me come in as a precaution. I only stayed overnight because my blood pressure was a little high."

My father looked at the monitor above my head. "Pressure's nice and low now. Machine took it while you were sleeping."

I let out a large exhale. "Oh good. Hopefully I can get out of here this morning."

I caught Dad up on everything that transpired last night. When I was almost done, there was a knock at the door. I turned to find Rush walking in with two coffee cups in his hand. He set them down on the food tray next to my bed and extended his hand to Dad.

"Mr. Mirabelli." Rush nodded, and my father stood to shake his hand.

"Call me Tony, son. And I really appreciate you calling. Especially since my *daughter* didn't think it was important to give me a ring."

Both men's eyes landed on me with serious faces. "No problem." Rush shook his head. "She didn't think it was important enough to call me, either."

I rolled my eyes. "*I was fine.*"

Rush nodded toward the coffee on the tray. "That's a decaf for you." He looked at my dad. "You can take the other,

Tony. I already had one, and I can pick another one up on my way to work."

"Thank you."

The room became awkward all of a sudden. Rush shoved his hands into his jean pockets and looked out the window, seemingly lost in thought. Eventually, his focus came back and he glanced back and forth between Dad and me a few times. His face was sad. "I guess I should get going then. I have a seafood delivery coming this morning at the restaurant. I'll come back after."

My dad stood. "You go do what you have to do. I'll take it from here. No need to come back. Thanks again for calling me."

I didn't want Rush to leave, and it didn't look like he really wanted to leave, either. Or maybe that's just what I wanted to see. But he kissed me goodbye on the forehead, nonetheless. "Text me, and let me know you're home safe. Okay?"

I nodded.

He walked to the hospital room door and stopped. For a second, I got my hopes up that maybe he'd changed his mind. But instead, he looked back over his shoulder one last time and said, "Take care of yourself, Gia."

CHAPTER 12

Rush

I had two channels lately: pissed off and *really fucking pissed off*.

"I don't give a shit what you do with it!" I barked at one of my employees who had tried to ask me where he should put a case of champagne that had been delivered for the upcoming end-of-summer bash. "Just deal with it." At least it was only Rhys. That fucker was lucky he still had a job anyway.

A few minutes later, Riley walked over and told me she'd lost her apron and asked where to find another one. I glared at her until she scurried away with her tail between her legs. I should've fucking fired her a second time. Or maybe it was a third. I'd lost count.

Not long after, I was sitting at the bar working on adding up some invoices when Oak tapped me on the shoulder. "Boss. You have a visitor."

I didn't look up. "Tell 'em to fuck off! I'm busy."

It wasn't Oak's voice that responded. "I carry a gun. Not sure fuck off is a good answer to give me."

Shit.

Gia's father.

Just what I needed.

I turned around. "Sorry. It's been one of those days."

Tony chuckled and slapped me on the shoulder. "One of those days or three of 'em?"

I knew what he was getting at. After Gia got out of the hospital, I'd made her take a few days off as a precaution, even though the doctor had cleared her to return to work. It had been three days since I saw her—which happened to be the same number of days I had been fucking miserable. Tony was a cop. I didn't bother to try and lie to him. Instead, I stood and walked around behind the bar.

"What can I get you to drink?"

He held up a hand. "Just a seltzer would be great. About to drive back to Queens." Tony had stayed at Gia's rental since she got out of the hospital. It gave me a modicum of relief to know someone was looking after her, at least.

I poured a seltzer and slid it across the bar, then proceeded to make myself something a fuck of a lot stronger. "I'm not driving anywhere. Hope you don't mind, but something tells me that you showing up here alone…I'm gonna need it."

He smiled. "Have your drink. Come sit."

I finished mixing a vodka seltzer that was more vodka than seltzer, and took a seat on the stool next to Tony.

He reached behind his back into the waistband of his pants and pulled out a bag. Opening it, he dumped a stack of postcards bound together with a rubber band onto the bar.

I looked down at the pile. "Vacation souvenirs? You can probably pick up one in the drugstore in town if you're looking to add to your collection."

Tony shook his head. "No. Not vacation souvenirs. Well, not from any vacation I ever took, anyway. These are from Leah, Gia's mother."

Tony read the confusion on my face.

Removing the rubber band…he started to toss them one by one in front of me.

"Look at the postmark dates."

I picked up a few and looked at the worn ink. "All on Gia's birthday?"

"Yep. Every year on Gia's birthday, her mother mailed her a different postcard from a different place."

"She never mentioned that."

Tony stopped his one-by-one toss of the postcards and turned to look me in the eyes. "That's because she doesn't know. And I hope to keep it that way, if you catch my drift."

I nodded. "Understood."

"Anyway." He tossed a few more in front of me and kept one in his hands. "They'd come every year like clockwork. I know Leah's handwriting, so I knew they were from her, but they were always blank."

"Okay…"

"When Gia's mother left, she told me she didn't want to be pinned down with a child, that it was her destiny to travel and see the world. I'd met her while we were both vacationing down in New Mexico. We both had a bit of wanderlust in us. First year we got together, we saw fifteen states. After we got married, we planned to finish seeing the rest and start on Europe. We had big plans. We were saving money to take a year off and do nothing but travel." Tony paused to drink some of his seltzer, but I got the feeling he needed a minute, too. "Anyway, Leah got pregnant and that changed everything. At first, she was excited about it, thinking it wouldn't have to change our plans. But the reality of that hit real quick. I took the police test for a steady income and health insurance, and they called me right before Gia's first birthday. Leah stayed home with Gia. With a baby, money was too tight to travel. It wasn't what we planned, but life doesn't always go as planned, does it?"

"No, sir."

"Anyway, my daughter says I can turn a knock-knock joke into the Declaration of Independence, so I'll try to sum up and keep it brief this time. Leah didn't like the change of plans and took off one day, leaving a Dear John letter in her place. One of those postcards arrived in the mail every year, always blank, until Gia's eighteenth birthday." He tossed the remaining postcard in his hand on the top of the pile. It wasn't blank like all the others. I glanced down at it and back to Tony.

"Go ahead. Give it a read, son."

> *Dear Tony,*
>
> *This is the last postcard you'll receive. I've spent the last eighteen years traveling from place to place, looking for someone or something that I could never seem to find. Today it hit me. I've been looking for someone to replace you and Gia. I looked for pieces of you in every relationship I had. And in the end, nothing compared to the original. You've stayed in my heart far longer than you were in my life.*
>
> *Our daughter is a woman today. I hope she's like you. Strong enough to have the courage to deal with the unexpected and not run away when life turns out different than*

*planned. Take it from me, you can run away
from people, but you can't run away from
what's in your heart.
Always, Leah*

"Don't let eighteen years pass before you stop running,
Rush."

———

Tony had left me even more fucked up than I'd been before
he showed up. Only I wasn't angry anymore; I just felt down.
Like I'd lost my best friend, quit smoking, and someone had
run over my fucking dog—all in the same morning. He'd
obviously brought me Gia's mother's postcards to show me
that cutting the person out of your life doesn't always let you
move on. But the thing was, unlike Gia's mother, I didn't
think there was anything better out there for me that I needed
to search for. Gia was better than I even deserved.

Unable to focus, I got tired of sitting in my office. For
three days, I'd had Gia on the brain, and it was only getting
worse. I needed to see her, even if it was the asshole thing to
do when I couldn't give her what she wanted.

I stopped by the kitchen and had the chef make a bunch
of her favorite dishes, and decided to drop in and check on
her unannounced.

Twenty minutes later she opened the door, and I stood
staring at her, completely forgetting what my excuse for
coming by had even been. *God, she looked hot as fuck in
that bikini.*

"Rush? Is everything okay?" Her brows drew down with
concern.

I remembered the guise I'd come under. Holding up the bag, I said, "Thought you could use dinner. Did I interrupt you going for a swim or something?"

"No. I just sort of wear bathing suits around the house now because my clothes are too tight." She fingered the edge of her bikini bottom that was pushed down under her beautiful, plump stomach. "It's like walking around in my underwear, but socially more acceptable."

I'd forgotten what her curves did to me. Seeing her bare stomach with a little more fullness to it, her tits really filling out the top, I wondered if stopping by had been such a good idea after all.

Gia licked her lips. "I'm starving. Any chance there's eggplant in there?"

"Sure is."

She practically ripped the bag out of my hand and left me standing in the doorway as she walked away. I started to chuckle, but then got a look at her from the rear.

Damn. Not funny.

Maybe I should be like a deliveryman and bolt. The little T&A show was enough of a tip.

Gia yelled from somewhere in the house. "Rush? Where are you?"

I looked up at the sky and cursed myself for thinking this was a good idea before I walked in.

She had a fork out and two containers open by the time I walked the few feet to the kitchen.

"Hungry?" I raised a brow.

She stabbed her fork into a mini eggplant rollatini and shoveled it into her mouth. Closing her eyes, she practically moaned. "Mmmmm...this is so, so good."

I swallowed. "Yeah. Good."

Like a fucking perv, I stood there leering at her, thoroughly turned on from the noises she made while she devoured half a plate of eggplant. At one point, some sauce dripped onto her cleavage. She used a finger to swipe it away, then sucked on the damn finger.

Clearing my throat, I said, "Why don't you get some clothes on? A cover-up or something?"

She pouted and put down the eggplant. "Why? Because I'm fat?"

"Just the opposite, because you're killing me in that bathing suit."

Gia looked down at herself. "Oh." She seemed to get my point and retreated to her bedroom to put on a robe.

We sat in silence when she returned to the table and finished off the eggplant. I ate the scraps she didn't finish, which weren't much.

"I'm really hot. Must be all the spices in that dish. I'm gonna take off this robe now, okay?"

Yeah. I'm really hot, too, and it's most definitely not the spices in the dish.

She let the robe fall to the ground, and my dick immediately hardened. Her breasts were even bigger than they were the last time I'd seen her. Jesus Christ. How much bigger could they get?

Fuck. I want you so badly, Gia.

I was going to have to just suck it up. "Yeah. It's fine if you take it off."

Speaking of sucking, I would have given anything to bear my mouth down onto those hard nipples pointing through the spandex material of her bikini top. Trying not to touch her was pure hell. The swell of her smooth, tanned stomach was almost too much to take. That little dome with that perfect belly button. Even the disturbing realization that she was carrying Elliott's baby in there couldn't stop the fact that I was still jonesing for her body twenty-four seven. But whenever I was physically around her, that feeling was ten times worse. I couldn't imagine how I'd feel if it were my baby. I'd probably be even more turned on, if that were even possible.

I started a conversation to get my mind off this physical need. "How's the book coming?" *Coming*. My reaction to that simple word reminded me of that game I used to play with Gia at the bar.

"Believe it or not, it's coming along better than it ever has. I am in the middle of a sad part where the couple can't be together."

"Oh, so you turned it into an autobiography, did ya?"

That was a sad attempt at a joke on my part.

"No. It's just art imitating life." She smiled.

Even her smile set me off. I shut my eyes momentarily to curb the need to reach over and kiss the hell out of her.

"When do you think you'll be finished?" I asked. "I'm curious to read it, to see if you've written me in as a deviant side character."

"Oh, you've definitely made your way in." She laughed.

Lifting my brow, I said, "Yeah? What does that mean?"

"Well…since I can't have the real thing…I've taken to remembering sex with you and using it as inspiration for those scenes."

Fuck.

"You stealing my moves, Mirabelli? Isn't that copyright infringement?"

"Nope. You gave them to me. They're my moves now." She winked.

I would love to give it to you. Right this fucking minute.

"I just sent the first half of the book to my agent. A few of the chapters are really hot. She's gonna get an eyeful. I'm supposed to be going to the City in a few days to have lunch with her and talk about it, actually. I'm sure she'll let me know exactly how she feels about everything."

It made me happy to see that things were moving along with her writing. She'd struggled for so damn long. At least one thing was going right in our lives.

"Cool. Good luck with that."

"Thanks."

Figuring I could use a nice splash of cold water on my face, I got up to take a leak, deciding to use the bathroom outside of Gia's bedroom.

On my way out, I took a peek inside her room and noticed some boxes. The sight of that made my stomach sick.

I walked inside and looked around. This was serious.

When I returned to the living room, Gia's eyes were closed. It looked like she was nodding off.

"I see you picked up some boxes."

Her eyes flew open at the sound of my voice. "Um... well...I need to start slowly packing things away. I told you...I'm moving back to the City. And I might as well give you my two weeks' notice now, too. I'm leaving after the end-of-the-season party."

It felt like she'd hit me with a ton of bricks. The right words escaped me. She was giving me her notice. She was leaving. I knew this was coming. I had just been hoping to figure out a way to stop it. But could I really stop it? I knew

I wanted Gia in every way, but that seemed like a separate thing from whether I could be a father to Elliott's child. That was the issue I still hadn't figured out. And until I did…I didn't have the right to dictate her every move. Up until now, there hadn't been a timeline by which I needed to figure things out, but it seemed that was no longer the case.

I had two weeks.

CHAPTER 13

Gia

It was the middle of the busy lunch hour at the cafeteria-style restaurant. I'd just spent the last hour filling my literary agent, Talia Bernstein, in on all of my personal happenings of this summer. Talia was young and hip, so I didn't feel like she would judge me.

While I stopped short of confessing the Elliott connection, I told her I had gotten pregnant by a one-night stand, that I'd fallen in love with someone else before I knew about the pregnancy, and that the relationship was now in jeopardy as a result. Needless to say, despite how "cool" she was, her mouth was pretty much hanging open at how much I'd been through.

She shook a small packet before dumping the sugar into her coffee. "Well, it's no wonder you struggled with this storyline, because quite honestly…your life is much more exciting than the book. No offense…but Jeez Louise, the angst. I can't even imagine what you're going through right now."

"I wish I was only imagining it," I said before taking a sip of my water.

"Would you consider writing your story next?"

I squinted in confusion. "*My* story?"

"Yes. The story of this past summer. Girl moves to a summer share, gets pregnant by a one-night stand, falls in love with her sexy new boss who has to determine if he can be a father to the baby. What happens next? I don't know about you…but I'm dying to know." She leaned in. "I'll start pitching it to the Big Five tomorrow if you give me the okay."

My body stiffened. "You can't be serious…"

"I'm dead serious. Think of the perspective you could bring. And we could tout it as 'based on a true story'. People will totally eat that up."

"I don't think I could do that. I'm too close to the situation."

She laughed. "That's the point! Think of how easy it will be to pour out those words."

"I know…but what I mean is…it would just be too much for me. I think in many ways my current emotional state has been driving my recent material, though. Which is a good thing."

"Oh, well, yes, that's evident. The emotion in the last few sections—the chapters where they have been apart—was exactly what I was looking for. I have to tell you…I was so pleased with those parts. I feel like where we were at the beginning of the summer when you were struggling with where to take the characters beyond those first few chapters compared to now…it's night and day." She took a sip of her coffee, then sighed. "Gosh, I still wish you would consider putting pen to paper about your summer experiences. I think it would make an amazing story."

Now I became a bit defensive. "Some things are sacred, Talia. I wouldn't dream of exploiting what I have with Rush. Can you understand that?"

She looked like she regretted her earlier statements. "You know what? You're totally right. I just got a bit excited. It's your life. Not a book. I get it."

"That's okay." I played with my straw. "That's not to say there aren't parts of Rush that made it into this book."

Talia's eyes lit up. "I take it he inspired the sexy times?"

My face felt flushed. Was I being bashful? For a woman pregnant with her boyfriend's brother's baby, you'd think nothing could affect me anymore.

It was a beautiful, sunny but cool day in Manhattan. After my lunch with Talia, I happened to be walking down Madison Avenue when I came across a photography studio. In the window were gigantic photos of the most gorgeous babies—very reminiscent of Anne Geddes with bright colors and animal themes.

There were also some pregnancy portraits. A black and white photo of a very pregnant woman wrapped partially in a silk bed sheet while exposing half of her bare stomach caught my attention. She had long, flowy hair and was really quite gorgeous.

I decided to walk in and peruse the place. Maybe it was the hormones, but I couldn't refuse anything lately that had to do with babies.

"Can I help you?" the woman asked.

"Oh no. Just browsing. You have a gorgeous studio. The portraits in the window really drew me in. I just had to come see more."

"Are you expecting?"

"Do I look like I am?"

"No. I'm conditioned to ask everyone that question."

"Actually, yes, I am." I smiled.

She looked down at me. "Ah…I see it now."

I shrugged and rubbed my stomach. "Yeah, I guess I can't really hide it anymore."

"Are you interested in a shoot?"

Her question caught me off guard. "Oh…I don't know. I really don't think I'm ready for that."

"Well, I'm booking six months out now. So you could always schedule something and then see if you're interested when the time comes."

"Really? That far in advance?"

"Yes." She smiled proudly. "I'm fortunate to be in high demand."

"Well, I can see why. You're very talented. That one over there with the butterflies is so adorable. They all are, really. I couldn't choose one."

My eyes wandered over to a baby with wings, and that, of course, immediately reminded me of Rush's winged women. I sighed. *He's so complex and amazing.*

"Take a look around," she said, walking back over to her desk to give me some space.

I kept looking at all of the cherub-like baby faces around me. A fleeting thought that my baby could look just like Elliott, with his blond locks and maniacal grin flashed through my mind. I was sure I'd still love my child just the same, but it was strange to imagine him or her resembling Elliott. I couldn't even think about how hard that would be for Rush.

The woman interrupted me. "Want to take a look at the price chart…in case you're interested?"

I hardly thought I would be able to afford this once the baby came, but you couldn't put a price on good photography. It was essentially buying memories. Maybe I could book the shoot now and figure it out later.

"You know what?" I nodded my head once. "Sure. Is there any fee for cancellation, though?"

"No. We just like as much notice as possible."

After browsing the different packages, I chose one in the middle of the price range.

After I gave her my name to book it, she said, "Gia Mirabelli…that's strange."

"Why?"

"Someone by that exact name is already scheduled." She scratched her chin. "Wait…I remember this. He booked a pregnancy shoot and then an infant shoot for later. Seemed so in love with the woman."

"He?"

"Yes. I could never forget this man. Very striking. Dangerous looking with a heart of gold. Rush was his name." She lifted her brow. "Know him by any chance?"

My pulse sped up. "Rush? He was here?"

"He's yours?"

There was something about that question that ripped my heart apart.

He's yours?

Because I couldn't say yes anymore. And I wasn't sure if he'd ever be mine again. Suddenly all of the hopes and dreams I once had, the ones I'd buried as of late, came flooding back to my mind.

Rush would have been the best father.

And he *wasn't* mine.

Tears were forming beneath my lids.

"Is everything okay?"

"We're not exactly together anymore."

"Oh...I'm so sorry. I didn't mean to upset you."

"It's okay." I wiped my eyes. "When did he make that appointment?"

When she told me the date, I nearly fainted. It was the same day he was in the City with Elliott. The day Elliott told him he'd slept with me. The day Rush figured out the truth. The day before that woman answered his phone. I cringed at the thought of what happened that night.

"Do you want to keep the appointments that Rush made?"

I seemed to have fallen into a daze now. "Sure. Yeah. Thank you."

On the way out, I couldn't help picking up my phone and dialing him as I walked down the sidewalk in a haze.

Unfortunately, it went straight to voicemail, so I left a message.

"Hey. It's me. You're never gonna believe this. By chance, I just walked into the same photography studio where you made me that appointment. I guess you never had an opportunity to tell me about it, or you may have forgotten with everything that's happened." Overcome with emotion, my voice was shaky. "Anyway...I went to make an appointment, only to find that I was already in the system. That was really sweet of you to want to do that. It's just another reminder of why I..." I hesitated and breathed, "Of why I love you.

I'll always love you, Rush. I hope you know that. No matter what happens…that's the one thing that won't change."

CHAPTER 14

Rush

Hearing Gia's quivering voice in that message really got to me. I stopped myself from calling her back, though, because I knew damn well what I wanted to say. I wanted to tell her that I loved her, too. But that would've been leading her on. I couldn't do that to her, even though I really did love her so damn much.

Things at The Heights were crazy. There were too many arrangements that had to be made for the end of the season and not enough hours in the day. In a sense, though, throwing myself into work had been a good thing. I needed a distraction from the memory of Gia's empty room, of her plans to leave town.

"Hey." Oak snuck up on me in my office.

"You scared the shit out of me."

"Yeah, well, you're easy to rattle these days, boss."

"What do you need?"

"Don't you think it's time you told me what the hell is going on with you and Gia? How could things be so great between you two and then turn to shit overnight? Something happened, and it's not making sense. She's having your baby, for Christ's sake. What could be so bad that you're letting her leave to go back to the City?"

My blood pressure was rising. I really did want to be able to tell him the truth. But it was just so goddamn painful to talk about. But so far, only my mother knew. If I was going to make a decision, I really did need to talk about it with someone I trusted. If I was being honest, Oak was one of the few people I could really trust. There was no reason not to open up to him, other than it was hard for me to rehash everything.

I decided to tell him.

Gesturing to the chair across from my desk, I said, "Oak…sit your big ass down."

He just kept saying, "Holy shit, boss. Holy shit."

Waving my index finger at him, I said, "If you ever tell a soul, Oak, there will be hell to pay."

"You don't have to worry about that. You know that. That's why you told me. Because you know I won't say anything."

I'd spent the past fifteen minutes telling him the entire story and the truth about Elliott. I couldn't believe that he was actually partly blaming himself.

"I remember the night Elliott was here," he said. "The asshole was walking around like he owned the place. I should have found a way to kick him the fuck out before he got to Gia. Then none of this would have happened. I never saw him with her, though. Must have lost track of him by that time. He got lost in the crowd of preppy dicks."

I couldn't help but laugh a little at his comment. "I wish you had kicked the fucker out, too, but it's not your fault. I hope you know that."

Oak cracked his knuckles. "I want to kill him. Seriously. That's how I feel right now. This situation is unbelievable." He crossed his arms. "What are you gonna do?"

Shaking my head, I sighed. "I wish I knew."

"I totally get it now…why you went away. It never made sense to me, how you could leave Gia while she was pregnant and just take off. Now it makes total sense. That must have been so hard for you, but I see why you had to do it."

"Yeah…why I went off the deep end." I rubbed my temples. "I wish there was a simple solution."

He was staring at me like he was considering something important. "Well, there sort of is."

Looking up at him, I said, "Oh yeah? Enlighten me."

"Well, it all depends on how you look at the situation. Everything in life is perception, right? Over time you might learn to accept that baby as simply Gia's, not Elliott's. But really, it comes down to one simple question. And I'm telling you…if you can answer this, then you have your answer."

"What's that?"

"You have to figure out whether your love for Gia is stronger than your hate for your brother."

———

Well, wasn't that a fucking question to ponder? Oak's words were playing in my head, haunting me, long after our conversation ended.

I was the only one left at The Heights as I locked up that night. The cool night air hit my face as I rushed to my car and grabbed the emergency pack of cigarettes I'd stashed in my glove compartment.

I held the pack in my trembling hand for the longest time and just stared at it. It felt like I was ready to lose it, give in to my need to smoke. Finally, I just crushed the package in my palm and threw it on the floor of my car. I'd come too far to start smoking again, even though I felt like I could have killed for a cigarette.

———

Returning to my house, I did something I hadn't done since finding out the truth: I opened the door to the nursery I'd built for the baby.

Everything sat untouched: the rocking chair in the corner, the crib, the mobile. It was stocked and ready for an infant who might never see it.

I sat in the rocking chair as I leaned my head back against the pillow and decided to return Gia's call from earlier.

She answered on the first ring. Her voice sounded a little groggy. "Hello?"

"Hey."

"Hi. I didn't think I would hear from you."

"I know. I'm sorry I didn't call you back. I just…wasn't sure how to respond to your message."

"That's okay. You didn't have to respond."

"Did I wake you?"

"No. I was just sitting in bed thinking."

My heart started to beat faster as I pulled on my hair. "You said I didn't need to respond. But I do, Gia. Because you told me you loved me, and I never even fucking called you back. I'm sorry."

"It's okay, Rush."

My voice sounded pained. "I love you, too. I really do. You know that, right?"

"I know. Your actions have always proven that."

"This is just so fucking hard," I breathed out. "This is the hardest thing I've ever had to deal with in my life. And I've been through some serious shit. But nothing compares to this."

"I know." She paused. "Where are you right now?"

"I'm home. I'm in the baby's room, actually. It's the first time I've let myself look at it since..."

She exhaled into the phone. "Oh, Rush. It must be strange to be in there."

"Nah…actually…it's kind of calming in a weird way. The dim lights. The baby stuff. The moon décor. It's just what I needed tonight, I think."

After some silence, she asked, "How was The Heights?"

"Boring without you, but busy with end-of-the-season shit."

"I can't believe the season is over."

"Yeah. It's always a stressful time." I paused. "Hey…so I told Oak everything tonight. About Elliott, too. I thought you should know."

There was some silence before she responded, "Oh. Okay."

She sounded weird about that.

"Is that okay?"

"Yeah, of course. Just took me a second to process it. I trust Oak. He's a good guy, and you needed to talk to someone. What did he say?"

"He gave me some good advice. Some stuff to think about. He really likes you, Gia."

"I really like him, too. I'm gonna miss him."

I hated the reminders that she was leaving.

"I almost smoked tonight," I said. "Really close to falling off the wagon but caught myself."

"I'm so proud of you for keeping that up. I know it can't be easy with everything that's been going on with us. But it makes me feel good to know you're not filling your lungs with that crap anymore. I don't ever want anything bad to happen to you."

Grabbing a stuffed elephant off the nearby dresser, I clutched it to my chest. "This whole thing with us, Gia...it isn't a decision you make overnight. I wish it were simple. I wish I could sit here and say with one hundred-percent certainty that I knew I could handle it. All I know for sure is that I love you and care about this baby enough to really think about whether I can be the kind of father he deserves under the circumstances. I will not look at him with resentment the way my father looked at me. I can't do that to him. I won't. I love him too much, if that makes sense."

"I know. I get it. And I totally understand your need to think this through. It's why I'm leaving to give you space. It's the best thing right now. Plus, my dad has been really supportive, and I think I just need to be closer to him right now."

It hurt me that she felt she needed him more than me...but then I had to remind myself that I was basically pushing her away in a sense. My lack of answer was speaking volumes, even if I wasn't saying anything. What the fuck did I expect?

"I'm so sleepy, Rush. This baby is really kicking my ass."

"Why don't I let you go to bed?"

"I don't want you to go," she insisted. "Please...don't go."

Those words. Their meaning extended beyond tonight, and I knew it.

"You want me to stay on the phone with you?" I asked.

"Yes. I just want to hear you breathing while I fall asleep. Is that okay?"

"Yeah. Yeah, we can do that."

Resting my phone against my cheek, I laid back farther into the chair and closed my eyes, never imagining that Gia and I would be sleeping together this week.

But that was exactly what we did.

CHAPTER 15

Gia

It had become a game of sorts.

Make Rush Look.

It started out innocently enough. Earlier in the evening, I'd caught him watching me while I sat at my station inserting the daily specials into the plastic menu casings.

I smiled and waved. He lifted his chin giving me the casual Rush *what's up* and quickly looked away. The next few times I caught him, he diverted his eyes pretending that he hadn't been staring. And so my game began. A little extra wiggle in my walk. Licking my lips while I *innocently* looked down. Since I'd enjoyed myself so much for the first half of my shift, I decided to play the *advanced* version of *Make Rush Look* for the second half:

Make Rush Hard.

This wasn't a game for novices. A certain level of skill was required. And it was definitely for ages eighteen and over. Rush had disappeared to his office a little while ago, and I'd grown impatient for my turn. So I decided I should grab the extra salt from the storage room across from his office. None of the shakers were near empty, but I was a damn diligent employee. As luck had it, Rush's door was wide open, and the oversized container of salt was all the way down on the bottom shelf.

Like everything else I owned, the skirt I wore tonight was pretty damn tight. I held my breath and hoped that the fabric didn't split in two when I bent over without bending at the knees. I wanted to shove my big ass in his face, not ruin one of the few things that still fit me.

Even though the salt was right in the front, I spent a good thirty seconds moving things around on the bottom shelf while wiggling my ass. I was so damn obvious; I practically cracked up while I did it. All the blood had rushed to my head, so when I stood up I was a little lightheaded. I couldn't hide the smirk on my face as I wondered if all the blood had rushed to Rush's head, too—*his southern head*, that is.

I glanced across the hall and found Rush sitting in his chair, staring straight at me.

Two points for Gia.

Feeling particularly ballsy, I turned back around and quietly unbuttoned the top two buttons of my silky blouse. The material parted down to beneath my bra. Then I grabbed a stack full of extra menus that I didn't need from the top shelf and *accidentally* dropped them all over the floor when I turned around. I might as well have been naked from the peep show my gaping blouse gave when I bent to pick them up—one at a time, of course.

The look on Rush's face when I stood made me feel like a queen. But when he quickly diverted his eyes like he'd been doing something wrong, it caused a physical pain in my heart. Apparently, he hadn't read the rules to the game—*looking is encouraged*. So I decided to fill him in. He stared at my legs with every step I took from the supply closet into his office.

Shutting his door, I leaned my back against it with my hands tucked behind me. "You know, I see you watching me."

Rush clasped his hands together, resting his elbows on the arms of his chair—a very casual, but confident stance. Full of attitude. *So Rush.* "Is that so?"

I pushed off the door and took two steps toward him. "Yep. And you know what?"

"What?"

"I love that you look." I took another step. "I love that you don't seem to want to look, but you can't help yourself."

Rush just continued to stare at me. So I took that to mean he wanted to hear more. Raising my hand to the skin on my chest, I grazed a fingernail up and down my exposed cleavage. Rush's eyes followed along. "But you know what part I don't love?"

His eyes jumped to meet mine.

"I don't love that every time I catch you, you avert your eyes like you're doing something wrong. Like you're not supposed to be looking at me the way you do."

"Gia…" His husky voice was a warning.

So I took a few steps more and leaned on the opposite side of his desk, across from him. "Whether we wind up together or not, you're *supposed* to be looking at me. And I'm *supposed* to be looking at you the way I do. Because you're my person, Rush. And I'm yours."

His stare was so damn intense, but he still didn't utter a word. I walked around to his side of the desk and turned his chair so he faced me. "You do like looking at me, Rush, don't you?"

Still no answer, not in words anyway. But his breathing definitely said something. It grew louder, faster…heavier.

I scraped a finger along his chest. Between my legs throbbed with need, and I wanted nothing more than to get on top of his lap. What harm would that do? We were adults. He might not want to be together, but he clearly wanted me. It suddenly dawned on me that we'd been here before, with me taunting him and inviting him for a physical relationship, one with no strings attached. The only difference was—we had strings now. So many that we were both tangled and tied up with a million knots. But it didn't change the fact that we both had needs.

I unbuttoned another button on my blouse.

"Do you miss seeing me naked, Rush? Because I miss seeing your body. The hard lines of your stomach. The beautiful artwork inked all over. Your broad, strong shoulders. How hard you get for me…"

The air in the office grew so thick, it became difficult to breathe. Rush's eyes dilated to the point that he had little color left in his beautiful blues.

The muscle in his jaw ticked a few times. "What gets hard for you, Gia? *Say it.*" His voice was so damn raspy.

I ran my tongue across my top lip while he white knuckled the arms of his chair.

"*Say it…*"

"I love when your…"

A knock at the door cut me off. Rush's chest heaved up and down. He looked like he might burst if I didn't finish the sentence. But before I could speak again, a second knock came. This time louder, and the door creaked open a crack. "Boss. It's important."

Oak.

I quickly turned my back and buttoned my shirt. Rush adjusted his pants and pulled his chair closer to the desk to hide the very prominent bulge he was sporting.

"Come in."

Oak glanced back and forth between us and frowned. "Sorry to interrupt, boss. But you have a call. She called earlier, and I told her you were busy. But she called back again—said she's been trying to reach you, and you're not answering your cell. Said it's an emergency, or I wouldn't have bothered you two."

"Who is it?" Rush clipped.

"Lauren."

In a heartbeat, I went from hot and horny to frozen and freaking out.

Rush glanced up at me and lifted his cell from the desk. He scrolled, and we both saw a dozen missed calls and messages.

I swallowed.

Rush looked up at Oak who was still waiting at the door with the phone in his hand. "I'll take it in here."

He took a deep breath and picked up the cordless extension. Nodding to Oak that he was on, Oak clicked his extension off and backed out of the office.

"What's up, Lauren?"

I held my breath hearing her voice. I couldn't make out anything she said, but when Rush's eyes flashed up to meet mine, I thought I might pass out. *She knows. She knows!*

"Okay. Okay. Calm down," Rush said into the receiver. "And where's Elliott now?"

Oh God.

Oh God.

I'm not ready for this.

I really needed to sit down.

"Okay. I understand. I'm on my way. I'll meet you there in a little while. Try to relax. I'll take care of it."

He barely hung up the phone before I started shooting off questions. "What? What happened? He found out, didn't he?"

Rush closed his eyes for a few seconds and blew out a heavy breath. "No. It doesn't have anything to do with you or the baby. Elliott has apparently been down in Florida for a business meeting the last few days."

"What happened then?"

"It's Edward. They found him passed out on the ground in his office parking garage earlier. He's in the hospital. Apparently he had a brain aneurysm that no one knew about. He's on life support at Mount Sinai. They aren't sure if they can stop the bleeding or not."

"Oh my God." My hand flew to my chest. "I don't know what to say. I'm so sorry. What are you going to do? Head to the hospital?"

"I really don't think Edward would want me there. But Elliott can't get a flight back until tomorrow. Lauren sounded pretty nervous that he might..." He paused. "She doesn't want him to be alone. He has no other family, really."

As much as the thought of him spending time with Lauren scared the living shit out of me, I couldn't be selfish. I looked him straight in the eyes. "You should go, Rush. If you don't, it could be something you regret for the rest of your life."

Rush's face fell, but he nodded. He knew I was right. At certain times in life, the past doesn't matter, and you need to do the right thing as a human being.

"Do you want me to go with you? Riley is off tonight and didn't have any plans. I could call her to cover for me."

Rush looked conflicted as he searched my eyes. His instinct was to protect me at all costs. But I wanted to be there for him. Finally he nodded. "Yeah, I do."

―――――

My heart started to hammer inside my chest at the sight of Lauren in the waiting room. She stood as we approached.

"Thank you for coming. I didn't know what to do." Lauren hugged Rush and then turned to me.

"You, too, Gia." She hugged me and squeezed my hand. "I think our guys really need us right now."

I felt like the worst person on the planet. Lauren was so kind and caring, and here I was standing in front of her carrying her husband's baby, and she didn't have a clue. We'd passed a chapel down the hall on the way in, and I hoped she didn't want to go in there together to pray for Edward. I was certain my feet would combust.

The two of them talked for a while. Lauren filled him in on what she knew so far and then told him the doctor said two people could visit at a time.

Rush couldn't hide the stress that the thought of walking in to see Edward in ICU caused. I took his hand and squeezed tight. "I'll go with you."

We walked through the ICU doors like we were going to our own beheadings. Small steps and terrified. Edward's little area had the curtain drawn, and we heard people working on him. So we waited.

"Are you here for Eddie?" A heavyset nurse with an unexpected southern drawl asked.

I waited a few seconds for Rush to answer. When he didn't, I did. "Yes. How's he doing?"

She attempted to smile and stay positive, but I didn't need to know her to see she wasn't that optimistic. "He's holding his own. He's a fighter. I just cleaned him up. You can go on and visit. Don't let the tubes scare you too much." She took off a paper gown that she had worn over her uniform and crumpled it into a ball. "You must be one of his sons, right? I can see the resemblance."

Rush just kept staring at Edward in the bed, so I answered again. "Yes, I'm Gia, and this is Rush."

She stepped on the garbage can pedal next to her and tossed the disposable gown in. "I'll give the doctor a call and let him know you're here so that he can come speak to you."

"Okay. Thank you."

When the nurse walked away, Rush and I approached the bed still hand in hand. Edward looked frightening. There was a tube down his throat, a tube up his nose, and at least four bags of medicine running from an IV pole to his hand. A machine flashed all kinds of numbers to his left, while another machine hissed breaths into his body from the right. He looked so pale and weak.

Neither of us said a word as we stood there. At one point, I watched Rush close his eyes, and I thought he might have said a little prayer. Then he did something I never expected. He reached down and took Edward's hand. I had to swallow to keep my tears at bay.

The silence didn't break until a doctor broke it for us.

"Hello. I'm Dr. Morris." He extended his hand and shook both of ours.

"Rush. I'm Edward's…son. And this is Gia."

"Hi," I said, grateful that Rush had snapped out of it enough to converse with the doctor.

Dr. Morris nodded his head toward the nursing station nearby. "Why don't we talk over there?"

Away from Edward's bedside, he put his hands on his hips and sighed.

"So…your father was brought in with a ruptured aneurysm. In case you aren't familiar with the term, an aneurysm is basically a balloon-like bulge that pops out of an otherwise normal artery wall. Unfortunately, it's common that there are no symptoms of the bulge until it grows and the pressure becomes so much that it ruptures. Picture a straw with a small crack and an uninflated balloon sticking out of it. Over time, through the pressure of our blood pumping, the balloon starts to inflate until it becomes so full that it bursts. That's what happened to your father. It's called a subarachnoid hemorrhage."

"Okay. So his balloon gave way and now, what, everything that was inside goes where?" Rush said.

"That's half the problem. The blood releases into the space around the brain. It's essentially a hemorrhagic stroke and can cause some pretty severe damage, such as paralysis, coma and…worse. In some patients who make it to the hospital, the bleeding slows or stops by itself. Other times it doesn't, and the patient isn't stable enough when we go in and try to stop it. Your father's bleeding seems to have slowed, for the most part. Which is good, because performing surgery to open up his skull while he's in this weakened condition would pose significant risk for complications."

"It slowed, not stopped?"

"That's right. So now we're at a point where we need to weigh the risks of further complications from the slow bleeding, against the risk of bringing him into surgery to try and stop the bleeding altogether while his vitals remain this unstable."

"And which is riskier?"

"Unfortunately, the risk is pretty even. If we don't stop the bleeding, he could have further damage. Although we don't yet know what damage he's already incurred. But if we go in to stop it, there's a good chance he won't make it out of the O.R."

"Jesus." Rush dragged his fingers through his hair.

"What are you recommending?"

"My current recommendation is to hold off on the surgery, at least for a few hours to see how things go. We'll, of course, keep scanning him to look for any changes one way or the other. But you need to understand that there's a risk in waiting, as well. I'll need you to think it over, and give me some guidance on how you think your father would want to be treated."

We talked to Dr. Morris for another twenty minutes. Rush asked questions about potential outcomes to waiting versus having the surgery, including how Edward's quality of life might be. I don't think I would have been able to be in such a clear frame of mind had it been my father—or even my own estranged mother. But Rush pulled it together, and by the end of the conversation, he seemed well informed and said he'd speak to his brother and get back to him soon.

"It's a big decision," the doctor said. "Just have the nurse page me if you have any more questions."

"I will. Thank you."

The doctor patted Rush on the back and gave me a nod. As he started to walk away, Rush stopped him. "Doc?"

He turned back.

"Can he hear us? You had us step out to talk. So does that mean he can hear us?"

"We're not sure, son. Sometimes patients come out of it and remember random things that they couldn't have known without hearing. But most of the time patients don't recall having heard anything when they wake back up. Although that doesn't mean they aren't hearing you during their time out. I'd encourage you to try to talk to him. The benefits to both of you might be important."

"Thank you."

We went back to stand with Edward for a while and Rush remained silent. Considering he could possibly hear us, it wouldn't have been right to discuss what the doctor had said in front of him. Eventually a nurse came back over and said we'd need to step out in a few minutes so they could take some bedside X-rays, but we could come back again when they were done.

Rush nodded and said we'd leave in a minute.

He was quiet for a moment and once again took his father's hand. When he started to speak, at first I thought he was talking to me. But he wasn't. He was speaking to Edward.

"I know we never got along. You might not be happy that I'm even here right now. But your other son—Elliott—he needs you. On some level, I've always been jealous of what you and Elliott had. The connection the two of you share. So even though we might not be that close, I've seen with my own eyes how much he looks up to you. How much he loves you and needs you. So fight for that. Fight for Elliott, Edward." Rush paused for a moment, then added. "Plus, if anything happened to you, I'd have to find a new nemesis. And I'm not so great about change. So hang in there, you big pain in my ass."

Rush and Elliott decided to follow the doctor's advice and hold off on surgery. Later in the night, Rush talked Lauren into going home and getting some sleep, assuring her that he'd stick around and let her know if anything changed. He tried to send me home in an Uber, too. But there was no way I was leaving him. The nurses were kind and brought us two comfortable chairs that reclined a little so that we could sit by Edward's side in ICU all night. We both actually dozed for a few hours, and when we woke up it felt like one big do-over. The only thing that had changed was that light now streamed through the window behind his bed.

"I'm going to run and get some coffee," Rush said. "You want something?"

I patted my belly and smiled. "Yes. And I'm too lazy to get up and go with you."

He hit me with the first real smile I'd seen since before Oak walked into his office twelve hours ago. He stood and stretched his arms into the air, before walking around to where my chair was positioned. Leaning down, he kissed my belly and whispered in my ear. "I'll get both of you something to eat. Be back."

After he disappeared, I closed my eyes again and started to fall into a light sleep. Rush's footsteps approaching made me smile. They stopped next to me, and I still hadn't opened my tired eyes.

"Can you feed me? I'm too tired to do it myself," I teased and opened my mouth, figuring I'd get a dirty comeback from Rush.

But it wasn't Rush's voice that spoke.

"Open wider. I got something for you, alright."

Elliott.

CHAPTER 16

Rush

"**P**iece of shit." I kicked the damn vending machine that had just stolen my dollar. Thinking maybe it was just out of coffee, I pushed every other button. Of course, it didn't do anything except piss me off. When it ate my second single, I might've dented the thing.

Deciding a walk would do me some good, I made my way to the hospital main entrance and asked the security guard where I could get some coffee and breakfast outside of the building.

Last night after Gia fell asleep in her chair, I watched her sleep for a while. I couldn't stop thinking about the baby and what kind of a relationship Elliott might have with this child. And what the kid would think of Elliott. It got me thinking about Edward and me.

My whole life, all I wanted to do was hate the man. Hate him for what he'd done to my mother. But was he always an asshole? Without a doubt, I knew with absolute certainty that he had been a dick to me the last twenty years. Although I couldn't remember back when I was three or four. Had he tried back then, and it was me who never gave him a chance at all? Obviously, there are some situations that you never really understand unless you're part of them. I definitely recognized that better now that I found myself in a sharp corner of a similar kind of triangle.

At the deli, I ordered three breakfasts. An egg white omelet with turkey and Swiss for me, an order of French toast with whipped cream and a cherry for Gia—the whipped cream for her, the cherry for me to watch her eat it, and a giant cupcake with blue frosting for my little boy.

My little boy.

He really was my boy already. Beth was right. DNA didn't fucking matter.

In the span of the fifteen minutes it took me to go get coffee and breakfast, I'd gone from calm, to pissed off, and back to calm. People with real mood swings must be fucking exhausted all the time.

I saw Gia's foot tapping on the floor as I approached the curtain around my father's bed in ICU. I smiled to myself knowing she did that whenever she was anxious. My girl was anxious for food.

But the smile ripped from my face when I pulled back the curtain and saw Gia wasn't alone. Elliott was standing two feet away from her.

The burn of hatred heated my face. I wanted to beat the crap out of him more than I wanted anything else in the world at the moment. A stare-off ensued. I didn't give a flying fuck that he looked like he hadn't slept a wink in two days or that we were standing in front of a man he loved who was on his deathbed. My heart couldn't even consider those things; all it knew was that he was standing two fucking feet away from Gia—Gia, whom he'd been inside of—and I was about to explode.

My fist opened and closed, clenching at my side. I felt like a raging bull and, to me, Elliott was painted head to toe in the color red. I took a step toward him, but then something stopped me. Out of the corner of my eye, I saw Gia. She was white as a ghost and trembling in her chair.

Without giving my brother another thought, I went to her. I dropped the bag and took both her hands. "You okay?"

She nodded fast. Her hands stopped shaking inside mine. I looked down at them and then back to her. "You sure?"

"Yeah. Why don't I go wait in the waiting room and give you two a minute?"

"I'll walk you." Still ignoring my brother, I grabbed the breakfast bag, wrapped my arm tight around Gia's shoulder, and escorted her to the visitors' lounge. I knelt at her feet once we were there. "Did he say anything to you?"

"No. I just got nervous when he showed up."

I wasn't sure if she was telling the truth. My gut thought she might be lying, and Elliott had said something to her. Gia just didn't want me to make a scene. But right now, it didn't matter. As long as Gia was okay.

"He didn't touch you?"

"No! Not even a handshake."

I looked her over and let out a deep breath. "Fine. But you look exhausted."

"Thanks."

I brushed her hair from her face and kissed her forehead. "Eat. Your food is probably half cold to begin with. I'll go back in and deal with Satan while you feed our boy."

She gave me a soft smile. "Okay. But don't do anything to get yourself arrested. Because my father would probably show up here from the precinct in three minutes, and he'd kick your ass for leaving me stranded in the City."

My lip twitched. "Yes, ma'am."

"Promise me?"

"Fine."

On my way back to ICU, I looked over my shoulder and saw Gia already digging into the bag. I watched her lick her lips and tear into the Styrofoam containers and realized in that moment that nothing else mattered. Not even my asshole brother. So long as I could put that smile on Gia's face.

And then it hit me.

Something that Oak, of all people, had said to me.

"You have to figure out whether your love for Gia is stronger than your hate for your brother."

For the first time, I started to believe it just might be.

———

"Your opinion doesn't fucking matter."

I shook my head at my brother. The doctor had just walked out from ICU after giving me and Elliott an update on Edward's condition. He'd told us the morning scans had shown the bleeding had stopped, but they needed to keep him in a coma until the swelling in his head could go down. He wasn't out of the woods yet, but he'd taken a step in the right direction.

"The doctor asked us for our opinions," I said through clenched teeth.

"No one cares what you think. My father needs educated decision making. Did you even graduate from high school?"

"Let's not have this discussion near Edward. There's a possibility that he can hear every word that we say, and the last thing he needs is to hear us at each other's throats." I wanted to be at my brother's throat—with my hand crushing his windpipe—but I'd promised Gia not to get in trouble.

Elliott started to go off again, when Lauren suddenly walked into the curtained area.

"You made it." She smiled at Elliott. What the fuck did she see in him?

My brother's entire demeanor changed. A mask slid over his face, covering the contorted anger he wore for me. "Sweetheart. I'm so glad you're here," he said. I watched his entire act. Elliott morphed into the dutiful husband—hugging his wife like he'd missed her and kissing her on the cheek with a mouth that had undoubtedly been buried in some skank's pussy while he was down in Florida.

He wrapped his arm around her waist and held her close. Back to Ken and Barbie.

Unreal.

"How are you doing, Rush?" Lauren asked with genuine concern.

"I'm okay. But I think I'm going to head out since you two are back. Gia needs to get some rest. I'll probably just get a hotel nearby and come back this afternoon for evening rounds."

"That's crazy," Lauren said, looking at her husband. "They can stay in our guest room. Right, honey?"

Elliott flashed a politician's smile. "Of course."

Yeah, right. "Thanks, Lauren. But we're good."

"If you change your mind, or if Gia needs a change of clothes or anything, just text me."

I nodded and looked down at Edward one more time before leaving. "Call me if anything changes."

Every bone in my body ached from the intense muscle control it took to be around my brother and *not* beat the piss out of him. But I relaxed a little getting back to Gia in the waiting room.

"You want to get out of here?"

"But you didn't eat?"

"I lost my appetite."

She frowned. "You need to eat."

"Fine. Bring it. What do you think about getting a hotel somewhere close by so I can come back later for evening rounds to check on Edward? It's a hundred miles back to the Hamptons in traffic, just to turn around again. Unless you need to get back."

Gia stood. "I don't know…do I?"

I squinted.

"My boss can be a real prick sometimes. I'm supposed to work…"

I put out my hand to help her up. When she took it, I yanked her to her feet. "Let's go, wiseass."

"Can we stay at one of those three-hour motels? The ones that all the hookers use?"

"What the hell would you want to do that for?"

She shrugged. "Why not? It will be cool to people watch."

"And to lie in the same sheets that probably haven't been changed in a few weeks. Cum stains, blood, probably some shit streaks from dirty ass left behind, too…"

She crinkled up her nose. "Good point. Take me to the Waldorf Astoria."

"I was thinking more along the lines of the Hilton down the block."

"Cheapwad."

I shook my head. God, I fucking missed her.

"I wonder if he'll love peanut butter," Gia said.

My head rested on her chest. I'd been caressing her belly for the last twenty minutes while we talked in the dark. "If not, I'm not sure we can keep him. There's something off about people who don't like peanut butter."

She whacked me in the head. "Don't say my kid's going to be off."

"I didn't say that. Besides, he's your kid, so he's bound to be a little nutty. So you probably should get used to it now anyway," I teased.

"I hope he looks like my dad. Or you."

I'd never thought about it, but her kid *could* technically look like me. I shared DNA with his father. That thought reminded me of the act Elliott had put on for his wife. "Lauren seems like a nice lady. I just don't get how she can't see through his shit. One minute he was talking to me like I was garbage, and the next minute she walked in, and he became a different person. He has to slip up sometimes and show his true colors. You can't live with Dr. Jekyll and not see Mr. Hyde come out a few times."

Gia sighed. "I know you don't want to hear this. But I didn't see it. People see what they want to see. I was lonely and wanted to see Prince Charming who could change my current situation. Lauren doesn't want to see her husband for what he is."

"She's gonna find out the hard way…when he brings her home an STD instead of flowers one day."

Gia was quiet for a while. When she spoke again, her voice was a whisper. "Just so you know, I understand why you slept with that woman."

What the fuck?

I lifted my head from her chest and found her eyes in the dark. "What woman? What are you talking about?"

"That woman. Where did you meet her?"

"What woman?"

"The woman who answered your phone the night after you found out about Elliott being the baby's father."

Then it hit me.

"I met a woman at a bar, but I didn't sleep with her. What do you mean she answered my phone?"

"I called your phone the next morning and she answered. She seemed to know all about everything that had happened the night before."

I got up from the bed and turned on the light. Gia sat up, too. I was angry that she'd thought I'd done that all this time and never said a damn word.

"I shared shit with that woman while we got drunk—shit I regret sharing because it's private. She asked me to go home with her, and for a second, I thought about it. I wanted to hurt you back. But I couldn't do it. I stumbled to the parking lot, crawled into the backseat of my car, and passed out for the night. *Alone.* The next morning, I realized I lost my phone and waited until the bar opened to see if I'd left it inside. The woman had stopped by a few minutes earlier and left it with the bartender in case I came looking for it. *I don't even remember her fucking name.* You must've called while she had it." My blood was pumping at the thought that Gia had believed I'd cheated on her all this damn time.

"So you really didn't cheat on me?"

"I'd never cheat on you, Gia. And I'm pretty pissed that you thought I did and didn't call me out on it. You could be damn sure if some guy answered your phone when I called, you'd fucking know about it."

"What about the woman in Arizona?"

"Beth? Nothing happened with her either. She's an old friend with a great kid. I spent more time hanging around with him than her. Because in my fucked-up head it made me feel closer *to you* since you're pregnant."

"Oh my God. All this time…" Gia held her head in two hands.

"Why the hell didn't you *ask me* if you suspected something, anyway?"

"I…I felt like I'd deserved it, I guess. I'd hurt you and maybe a part of me wanted you to hurt me back. Plus…I didn't know if you being with another woman was cheating."

"*What*? You didn't know if me fucking another woman was cheating?"

She hesitated. "If you slept with a woman now, would you be cheating?"

"I just said I'd never cheat on you."

"But if you did, would it be considered cheating? In order for it to be considered cheating, you'd have to be committed to me." Tears built in her eyes. "I'm not sure what we are right now, Rush."

Jesus Christ. I'd really fucked with her head badly. She didn't even know that I would never sleep with another woman. I looked back and forth between her eyes and cupped her face into my hands. "I don't know where we're at right now either. How things will wind up in the future. I wish to God I could tell you that right now. But I do know one thing—you have me. There's no one else. Me being with another woman—or you with another man—would definitely be fucking cheating."

She started to cry. "Okay. I didn't cheat on you either. Not that anyone in his right mind would want me with what I look like these days. But I wouldn't do that to you, either."

I pulled her to me. "You do realize I'm sitting here with a hard-on, even in the middle of our arguing because I fucking love your body these days. So you saying *no one in their right mind would want you* is sort of insulting to us both."

She laughed through her tears. "I guess we're both a little crazy, then."

Truer words had never been spoken. After she had calmed down, I pulled back to look at her. "We good?"

She smiled. "Yeah. We're good."

"Okay. So can I shut the fucking lights off and get some shuteye? Because your ass snoring in the chair a few feet away kept me up last night."

"You're so full of shit."

I was. But I loved that she called me out on it. That was my girl. Not the one who thought I cheated and was too busy tiptoeing around my arrogant ass to say something. I got up and flicked off the lights.

It took a whopping five minutes for Gia to fall asleep once I pulled her to me, wrapped her tight in my arms, and stroked her hair. Me, I stayed awake longer, enjoying the feeling of being content for the first time in weeks, even in the middle of a shit storm.

CHAPTER 17

Gia

It sucked to have no money when you needed a new wardrobe. I knew Rush would have given me money in a heartbeat, but there was no way I was going to ask him.

But getting new clothes was becoming an urgent matter. That was what credit cards were for, I supposed.

Laughing to myself, I thought back to before I was pregnant and how I used to feel like I had nothing to wear, despite all of the clothes in my closet. It was certainly different when you *literally* had nothing to wear because you couldn't fit into a damn thing.

I found myself at the only maternity store in town. To my surprise, the woman behind the counter seemed to recognize me immediately.

"You're Gia from The Heights, right? Rush's girl."

Not really wanting to get into the whole "it's complicated" spiel with her, I simply said, "Uh…yeah. Yeah, I am."

It was interesting because I had no recollection of who she was. Yet, she knew me. That fact didn't surprise me. I'd been pretty oblivious to a lot of things at work lately, so preoccupied with my impending departure and the state of Rush and my relationship.

She held out her hand. "I'm Naomi, Rich Kirkland's wife."

Rich was one of the chefs at The Heights. Really nice guy and made the best teriyaki steak tips with mushrooms and peppers. Now my stomach was growling.

"Oh my gosh. We all love Rich. He's so sweet and such a damn good chef."

"Thank you. Yeah…he loves working there. When he got laid off from his other job, Rush heard about it and took him in, even though at the time they didn't even need another person. So we'll always be grateful for the chance he gave Rich."

"Wow. I never knew that."

That wasn't the only story like that about Rush. He often helped people in need. It was one of the things I loved about him.

She came around from behind the register. "So what brings you in today?"

I patted my belly. "Well, as you can see…I'm pregnant. I can't fit into any of my clothes anymore. And with this being the only maternity shop in town…I figured this was the place to be for expanding people like me. I need to find at least three staples that I can rotate. I'm a bit tight on funds, so stuff I can wear with a lot of different things."

She rubbed her chin as she walked toward the back of the store. "Okay, so then we'll mainly want to stick with bottoms. With tops you don't really need to buy maternity… you can go to Target and just get some looser fitting shirts."

"That's true. So maybe a couple of pairs of pants to start, not sure what selection of jeans you have?"

Naomi walked me around and helped choose a pair of dark blue jeans, a pair of basic black pants, and some maternity shorts. Even though I said I wasn't going to buy a shirt, I couldn't help picking one off the rack to try on. It was periwinkle blue with a drawstring at the back.

"Let me set you up in a dressing room," she said, leading me into one of the back stalls.

I slid the curtain open and hung my items on a hook.

"Holler if you need anything," she said.

"Thanks." I closed the curtain.

I blew out a breath as I just stared at myself in the mirror for a bit. Slipping my dress over my head, I was truly shocked to see how much I had popped. I rarely took the time to look at myself this closely—or at least not in this kind of stark, fluorescent lighting. It was really clear how fast this baby was growing inside of me. Depending on my mood, I could either look at myself and feel beautiful or fat. Whenever I thought about Rush, I felt beautiful. He made me look at all of the changes my body was going through as a good thing. Not sure I would be able to see the positive in all of this if he didn't constantly remind me how hot he was for me. Even the thought of that made my entire body tingle. Rush had control of my body even in his absence.

Good thoughts of Rush would always somehow evolve into worrisome ones. It was hard for me to feel fully confident about where things were going with us. Even though his behavior toward me lately made me optimistic, there was one major factor that caused me to doubt everything: he wasn't trying to have sex with me. It was the one thing he was holding back. It was clearly a conscious effort not to, given how horny he was. And it spoke volumes. Now that I knew he hadn't slept with anyone else, despite how much of a relief that was, it made me even more amazed and curious as to why he hadn't tried anything. Of course, that was enough to make me doubt all of the optimistic signs that he'd been showing lately.

Shaking that thought away, I slipped on the maternity jeans and somehow squeezed my ass into them. Once around my waist, they were pretty comfortable. I squatted to feel whether the material was stretchy enough. After I took them off, I tried on the other items before concluding that I'd be better off getting an extra pair of pants in a different color rather than the cute shirt.

Exiting the dressing room, I reluctantly returned the shirt to its rightful place on the rack, and Naomi helped me pick out a lighter pair of jeans in my size.

We took everything to the register. It seemed to be taking a long time for her to ring me up. She swiped the card several times and muttered something under her breath.

Naomi frowned. "You don't have another credit card, do you?"

"No. Why?"

"This one was declined. I tried it three times."

I was starting to sweat. Lately, I'd been charging a lot of baby stuff I was going to need in the future. It wasn't that hard to believe that my card could be near its limit. The payment I'd just made two days ago probably hadn't been applied yet.

Feeling embarrassed, I said, "You know what? I might have to call them and straighten it out. Don't worry about it. Now that I know what I like…I'll just come back and pick them up another time."

"Are you sure? I could probably do like a layaway plan if you want to put some money down."

The word layaway brought me back to flashbacks of going to T.J. Maxx as a child and depositing money toward my school clothes with my dad. That felt like just yesterday. Somehow pink and purple corduroys came to mind. Dad always found a way to get me what I needed even if it took some time.

I sighed. "No. That's not necessary. I'll straighten this out and come back."

Naomi flashed a sympathetic smile. "Okay. Sorry, it didn't work out, Gia."

"Me, too."

I walked out of there so fast. Feeling defeated, I decided to just go straight home and open a pint of Ben & Jerry's.

My plan was thwarted when my car struggled to start. I kept turning the ignition, and it just wouldn't budge.

Banging my hands repeatedly against the steering wheel, I yelled, "Are you fucking kidding me right now? You're gonna pick *this* moment to crap out on me? Thanks a lot you, you piece of shit!"

Whack.

Whack.

Whack.

My shoulders were rising and falling. Finally, I leaned my head against the steering wheel and just breathed, immediately feeling sad for being too hard on my car. That was an odd thing to be sad about, but nevertheless, I was. It was old and probably needed to just die, but I kept insisting it live, expecting it to perform as it used to. That was an unreal expectation. Who was the bad one in this equation? Me. I was. I cried thinking about that—about life and death. The death of things. The death of people. The death of relationships. Yes, my current sensitivity was probably the direct result of pregnancy hormones, coupled with the humiliation of my credit card problem, but still.

Taking one last deep breath, I exited the car and gently closed the door. Two minutes ago, I might have slammed it shut, but my sudden kinship with my broken-down vehicle meant that I had to be compassionate.

I patted the hood. "Sorry."

It was tempting to call Rush, but I stopped myself. It was imperative that I got used to doing things for myself and for my baby. That didn't include jumping to call Rush the second something went wrong.

So I began the long trek home by foot. Thankfully, the weather wasn't too hot, or else I would've worried about overheating in my condition. But it was just perfect, cool with a slight breeze.

An hour later, I was still walking, the bottoms of my feet sore and tired. Even my Tieks flats, which were super comfortable, couldn't protect me from succumbing to the harsh pavement.

At one point, a vague sense that someone was following me registered.

When I looked to my side, Rush's Mustang was slowly moving alongside me, just like he used to do in the early days of driving me home from The Heights.

He rolled down the window. "Why are you walking along this road, Gia?"

I was still moving as I answered him, "My car broke down."

He nudged his head. "Get in."

Picking up my pace a little, I walked backwards and said, "I don't want to, Rush. I'm trying to handle things as I would if I were living alone in the City, and you wouldn't be around to pick me up. So I'd like to walk."

"Gia…"

"Yeah?"

"Get the fuck in the car."

Well, I suppose I could blame my feet. They were practically crying for me to stop. Okay, I did really want to get in.

I shrugged and opened his passenger side door.

"Thanks," I said.

He placed his hand on my knee. "You crazy girl. You should've called me." My body immediately reacted to his touch. God, his hand felt good. *Move it just a little to the right.*

"I didn't want to bother you," I said.

"You should know that's not a good enough excuse and that I would drop everything to pick you up."

"I know you would. But that wasn't the point."

"The point was stupid."

I didn't want to argue with him. "Okay. Well, thank you for the ride."

He glanced over at me and lifted his brow. "Where were you coming from?"

"I was trying on clothes at the maternity store."

"Just trying them on?"

"Yes. I didn't buy anything."

"Why not?"

I didn't want to tell him the truth, but I couldn't lie. "My card was declined."

His expression dampened. "I see."

I sighed. "What are you thinking?"

"Nothing."

"Yes, you are."

"Well, I'm mad that you didn't invite me to come watch you try them on, to be honest." He flashed me a sexy smirk. One little look from Rush always went straight between my legs.

I turned my body toward him and lowered my voice. "You know, I was thinking of you when I was in the dressing room."

He smiled mischievously. "Oh, now this is a story I want to hear."

"I was thinking about how good you always make me feel about my body. The only reason I feel sexy right now is because of you. When I look at myself, I hear your voice telling me how hot I am."

"I don't do it to make you feel good. I do it because I genuinely love your body. If it makes you feel good, though, then that's an added benefit." He exhaled, his voice sounding needy. "So tell me about this trying on stuff. Were your tits bare?"

"No."

"Damn."

"But they were busting out of my bra, which is now too tight."

"So are my pants now." He groaned then glanced down at his crotch. "Thanks a lot."

"You're hopeless," I laughed, secretly loving that I was turning him on with my words.

"Will you let me watch next time?"

My body was heating up. "Are you serious?"

"Look fucking down. Do I look like I'm kidding?"

I laughed. "No, you don't."

"Okay, then. Next time you go clothes shopping, I wanna come."

Hearing him say he *wanted to come* made me have to clench between my legs.

When we arrived at my house, I turned to him after he shut the car off. "Did you want to come in?"

"Actually, I have to get back to The Heights. I have a lot of end-of-the-season stuff I've gotta get done."

I swallowed in disappointment. The old Rush would have taken any opportunity to jump my bones after the foreplay of our sexy conversation.

I simply nodded and exited the car.

He suddenly walked to the back of the vehicle and opened his trunk.

Rush took out three shopping bags. I recognized the name of the maternity shop on them.

Squinting my eyes in confusion, I asked, "What are those?"

"Your clothes. The ones you couldn't buy."

Pointing my index finger back and forth, I frowned. "How did you…"

"I didn't find you by chance. Naomi called me after you left and told me what happened. She said I might want to come and pay for my girl's stuff because she left upset after her credit card was declined."

I covered my mouth. "Oh my God. I can't believe she did that."

"I saw your piece of shit car still parked there and wondered if it had given you trouble. After that, sure enough, I found you walking along the road."

I looked through the bags. There were a ton of clothes. "I only had a few items I was going to buy. What the heck did you get?"

"I told her to give me everything she had in your size."

My mouth fell open. "I can't accept this, Rush."

"Yes, you can and you will."

"No."

"Gia…I'm not taking anything back. I like supporting local businesses. And if you don't wear this stuff…I will."

What?

Did he just say what I thought he did?

Bending my head back, I laughed at the ridiculousness of that thought. "*You're* gonna wear the clothes…"

He scratched his chin. "If you refuse them? Sure."

"Well, that's reason enough not to take them." I started walking back to my door, leaving the bags on the ground.

When I turned around, Rush had lifted off his shirt. I gasped inwardly at the sight of his cut chest. It had been a while since I'd seen it bare, and I swear, he looked hotter than ever.

Rush bent down and took the first thing he grabbed out of the bag. It was a pink, floral top. After examining it like he didn't know what hole to put his head through, he slipped it on. He then unzipped his jeans and kicked them off. I gawked at his muscular legs before he covered them with one of the maternity skirts.

With his hands on his hips, he winked. "How do you like me now?"

I love you.

I absolutely freaking love you.

The sight of this big, beautiful, tattooed man in that feminine ensemble was truly something.

"Only you could still look sexy in a pregnant woman's outfit."

"Don't make me have to walk into The Heights like this. Put me out of my misery."

My mouth hurt from smiling. "Okay, I'll keep the clothes."

CHAPTER 18

Rush

How many times was I gonna fix this crap car? I'd been under its fucking hood more than I'd been under Gia.

The day after I picked her up on the side of the road, I'd gone back to where it was parked in front of the maternity shop to try to get it running again.

At this point, getting it to run was like a battle against an enemy, and there was no way I was going to let this piece of junk win. I think fixing it repeatedly was like a challenge to me. That had to be the only reason I continued to mess with it, especially when it would have been much easier to just replace it.

After about an hour, I finally got it running. My plan was to drive it to Gia's and walk back to my own car.

Halfway there, the damn thing started smoking like crazy. I'd finally reached the end of the line. This was the last straw.

Breaking out into a laughing fit, I pulled over and leaned against it, buried in a cloud of smoke. Then, as if a switch went off inside of me, I began kicking the shit out of the car— over and over. This moment must have been the culmination of all of the stress I'd been under over the last several weeks.

But it just felt so damn good to do it. Add to that, the fact that I was picturing Elliott the whole time I destroyed this thing, and it was exactly what I needed. People were driving by and honking, but I didn't care.

After about five full minutes of beating the crap out of the car, I'd wrecked it beyond repair from a physical standpoint.

I just kept staring at it, and realized that this finally gave me an excuse to do something I'd wanted to for a while: buy Gia a new and reliable mode of transportation. The best part was she really couldn't refuse it. It wasn't like I was doing her a favor. I'd destroyed her freaking car, for Christ's sake. She had no choice but to accept a new one as a token of my apology.

Sweaty as all hell and feeling beat from my outburst, I walked the rest of the way to Gia's house.

When she opened the door, she said, "You look like you've been through hell and back."

I laughed, moving past her. "I was just in a fight."

"A fight?" She shut the door and clutched her chest in a panic. "With Elliott?"

"No…uh…" I chuckled. "With your car."

"My car?"

"I sort of trashed it. Went apeshit on it."

"What? I thought you said you were fixing it?"

"Well, I was. And I did. But then the damn thing broke down again and started smoking on the way home, and I lost it. Kicked the shit out of it, and now it's gone."

Her eyes were wide. "Gone? I don't have a car anymore?"

"Correct. It needs to be junked."

Gia's mouth was hanging open. "I don't know whether to laugh or cry."

"We'll go tomorrow and get you a new car."

"What? Just like that? You say it so casually like that's not a big deal. I can't afford to buy a new car."

I sat down at her kitchen table and kicked my feet up on a chair. "Gia…I *trashed* your vehicle. It's my responsibility to replace it."

"Well, you don't replace a used car with a new one."

"I don't want you driving the baby around in something unreliable."

She crossed her arms and blew air up to her forehead, looking frustrated.

Then I said, "I'll tell you what. I'll handle the down payment to make up for destroying your car. You can cover the monthly payments."

"No."

"Yes."

"No."

After twenty more minutes of arguing, she finally agreed.

I suddenly got up and smacked my hands together. "Good. I'll pick you up tomorrow morning."

———

Gia was shocked that I'd taken her to the Mercedes dealership. I wasn't going to buy her anything I didn't consider to be the safest possible option, and I'd done my research over the past twenty-four hours.

She kept saying she could never afford the monthly payments on a Benz. I reminded her that I was handling the down payment. That didn't mean it couldn't be a large amount of money—a small detail I neglected to discuss with her. I assured Gia she'd be left with a reasonable monthly bill. *Very reasonable.* Like almost nothing.

She was wearing one of her new maternity outfits, and this particular one hid her stomach and accentuated her tits. The car dealer likely didn't even know she was pregnant. That gave him free rein to flirt like hell with her. I was ready to snap his neck because he wouldn't stop staring at her knockers. Not to mention, when he asked if we were married, her answer was, "No, he's my boss." *Little shit.* Then she winked at me after, and I wanted to just take her right on the goddamn showroom floor. I would've loved to do so much damage on the hood of one of these cars that I'd have no choice but to purchase it. She was teasing about the boss thing—sure—but that just egged Dealer Dimwit to flirt with her more.

"What can I show you next?" he asked her tits.

"Give us a minute," I snapped, placing my arm possessively around her.

We'd just come in from test driving the SUV, when I told her, "You wanna test drive the E-Class?"

Gia was mostly considering "practical" vehicles. I couldn't blame her because I had always rented those for her in the past whenever her car would shit the bed. But I couldn't help noticing how she lit up when we'd passed the E-Class convertible.

She shrugged her shoulders. "Why bother?"

"Because you seem to love it."

"I can't get a convertible with a baby."

"Why not?"

"Because it's not practical."

"In what way?"

"Well…there's no…space."

"You planning on having more than one kid anytime soon?"

She laughed. "No. But what about things like the stroller?"

I went in search of Dealer Dimwit. "Hey, can you pop the trunk of the E-Class open?"

After he did it, I peeked my head in and smirked as I looked back at her. "Looks like plenty of space for a stroller."

Her eyeballs were flitting back and forth. She still looked like she was searching for reasons why she didn't deserve to have the car she actually wanted.

"Let me ask you this…" I said. "Do you plan on chopping off your hair and wearing Mom jeans after the baby is born just because those things are practical?"

"Hell no."

"Then why do you need to sacrifice what you really want in a car? Besides, there's plenty of room. Believe me, I wouldn't let you get something too small."

Her eyes were glued to the shiny silver convertible.

Gia was caving. "I guess we can test drive it."

I winked. "That's my girl."

We went to take it out, and the dealer had some nerve trying to get into the passenger seat next to her this time.

I practically shoved him to the side. "Excuse me. I'll be sitting in the front. And if you look at my girl's tits again, not only are you gonna lose out on this deal, you're gonna lose a mouthful of teeth."

He swallowed and stayed quiet as he crawled into the backseat. Gia looked a little embarrassed, but my reaction shouldn't have come as a surprise to her.

I barely remembered that he was even there once we took to the road. Gia had turned into a little speed demon in this thing, and I was loving it. Her wild hair was blowing all over the place, and all I could do was stare at her and enjoy every second of it.

This car would be worth every damn penny if I got to do this all the time.

Turning my head around to look at the back, I envisioned a car seat there and got chills. If only I could figure out what the chills were trying to tell me.

CHAPTER 19

Rush

I'd finally caught up at work. Between the building project on the other side of town, the upcoming end-of-season party at The Heights, going back and forth to visit Edward, working on Gia's hunk of shit, and going car shopping, I had a mile-long list of shit to do. But I came in at the ass crack of dawn this morning and tackled most of it by the time the dinner rush started pouring in. This time of the year, with the end of the season fast approaching, we were always extra busy.

I went behind the bar to help Riley and Carly and took a drink order for a snobby silver spoon type standing with a woman way out of his league. He ordered a scotch. I carded him just to be a dick in front of his lady friend.

He grumbled as he dug his license from his wallet. "I've been standing here waiting for ten minutes, and I haven't seen one person asked for proof of age."

I looked at his license, checking out the address after the year of birth. *Dune Road*. Figures. Most expensive beachfront hood in the Hamptons. No wonder he's able to snag her.

"When a young person orders an old man's drink, half the time it means they're trying to act mature because they're not of age. You ordered a scotch on the rocks."

He snatched his license from my hand. "*Or*, they have taste. And we'll take a pinot noir."

Dune Road's lady friend gave me a flirty smile from behind him. *Yeah, I don't blame you, sweetheart.* I poured their drinks and hit him for an extra four bucks on his bill—my own personal douchebag tax. Of course, he paid with a black card.

When they were done, he told her he wanted to go out to the back deck. As he turned to walk away, his girlfriend leaned to the bar. "What's it mean the other half of the time?"

It took me a minute to realize she was referring to my comment that dudes who order old men drinks were under age *half the time*. I leaned close to respond. "The other half of the time, they're just douchebags." She laughed and followed her cash cow out back.

After helping a few more people, I noticed the bar started to slow down so I went to help our hostess. She didn't look like she had too much to handle, but her ass looked spectacular in the new skirt she wore tonight, and I thought I'd let her know about that.

"Is that a maternity skirt?" I snuck up behind her and spoke over her shoulder. "You look extra sexy tonight."

"It is. It's so comfortable and stretchy. I could probably fit you inside of it with me."

I wanted inside, alright.

"That sounds like a challenge. You know how much I like a good…" I halted mid-sentence seeing a familiar woman walk into the restaurant. *Is that Lauren?* At first I thought it was. But she didn't look like her usual put together self. She had on a baggy T-shirt and a pair of yoga pants, and when she took off her sunglasses her eyes were puffy and red. It wasn't until she saw me and started making her way over that I was certain it was even her.

Unaware of who had just walked in, Gia turned around because I'd trailed off. "Rush?"

"Shit."

"What did I do?"

"Not you. Lauren."

Gia's nose scrunched up. "Lauren?"

She heard the voice, before I could explain. "Hi, Rush," Lauren said. "I'm sorry to drop in unannounced. Can we talk for a minute?"

Fuck.

"Sure."

I squeezed Gia's shoulder and whispered, "You good?"

The look she gave me screamed anything but. I gave her another squeeze. "I'll be back. Hang tight."

Lauren and I went to my office. She was quiet until the door closed. "I'm sorry. I didn't know where else to go."

I pulled out a chair. "Take a seat. Whatever it is, I'm here. It's fine."

She looked down as she spoke. "Edward needs more surgery. You know they were hoping to take him out of the coma they have him in soon."

"Yeah. The day before yesterday they were hoping for the end of the week. They said the swelling had gone down a lot. Did something change?"

"Not in his head. That's still good. But they did some other scans today as a precaution and found another aneurysm in his stomach. It needs to come out. They want your consent to perform the surgery."

"Why my consent? That's Elliott's decision."

Lauren looked down again and wrung her hands. "Elliott's not been so logical lately. He's been…drinking a lot."

"Everything with Edward too much to handle?"

Her eyes rose up to meet mine. Tears pooled and her bottom lip quivered.

"What's going on, Lauren?"

"Elliott…he…he…" Unable to hold back anymore, she broke into a cry.

I handed her a box of tissues and pulled a chair next to her so I could rub her back. "It's okay. Take your time. I'm right here."

My heart was ricocheting off my ribcage while I waited to hear what she had to say.

Eventually she sniffled a few times and continued. "Last week…I went to his office to surprise him with his favorite dinner."

The minute she said *surprise him*, I knew what was coming.

"He'd been so stressed between running the office and Edward being sick. I wanted to cheer him up." She wiped her eyes and looked at me. "But he had someone already doing that for him. *Right there in his office.*"

Fuck. Such a goddamn lowlife.

"I'd suspected something was going on before. But I guess I just chose to ignore it and pretend he wasn't cheating on me."

I hung my head in shame of my DNA. "I'm sorry, Lauren."

"Thank you." After a few minutes of her telling me all the clues she should have picked up on, we rounded the conversation back to Edward's condition.

"So is Elliott against the surgery?"

"He hasn't been to the hospital in twenty-four hours. He's just been drunk and pounding on my door. I'd asked him to leave because I can't be around him right now. But I went up to visit Edward this morning, and apparently they've been trying to reach Elliott since yesterday, and he hasn't called them back. They need a decision now. I'm sorry to put this on you, Rush."

"No. Of course. It's Elliott's responsibility and mine. Not yours. I appreciate you coming to me. I'll head into the hospital. Do you know where Elliott is staying?"

"I'm not sure. He was snoring on the floor outside of our apartment late last night. But this morning he was gone. I'm going to stay at my parents' summer home in Montauk for a few days, so if you see him, tell him that he can use the apartment until I figure out what I'm going to do."

"Okay."

Lauren stood. I wished there was something more I could do to help her. She didn't deserve this shit. "Montauk is twenty minutes. If you need anything at all, even just to talk or to scream about Elliott, don't hesitate to call me."

She gave me a hug. "Thanks, Rush."

I opened the door to my office and she stopped. These days, I thought there wasn't much that could shock me. But God had to prove me wrong.

Lauren turned back. "I almost forgot. We didn't get a chance to tell anyone yet." Her hand went to her belly. "I guess it's not exactly happy news anymore. But...I'm seven weeks pregnant."

Gia rushed into my office the minute Lauren was gone.

"She knows, doesn't she?"

"No."

Her hand clutched her chest. "Oh my God, Rush. Did Edward...I'm so self-absorbed, I wasn't even thinking..."

"Edward's fine. I mean...he's not fine. But he's not dead. Why don't you take a seat?"

Some of the color came back to Gia's face as she sat down in my chair. I filled her in on the latest on Edward's medical condition and told her that Lauren had walked in on Elliott with another woman in his office. I left out the part about Lauren being pregnant. *One nightmare at a time.*

"So you need to head to the hospital?"

"Yeah. I need to think about whether I'm going to try and find my asshole brother or not. But I'll have two hours in traffic to figure that shit out."

"I'm going with you."

I smiled, loving that she wasn't asking permission. "Yes, ma'am."

Oak called a friend to work the door so that he could pull double duty as manager and hostess. Ten minutes later, Gia and I were out the door. When we got inside my car, she was still lamenting over the news I'd shared.

"I feel so bad for Lauren. She looked awful when she ran out. I hate to say it, because I'm certain she's in a lot of pain right now...but she's better off finding out now about Elliott. It would be so much harder for her to go through all of this if they had a family."

I hesitated to put the key into the ignition. *Crap.*

"What's wrong?" Gia asked.

I shifted in my seat to face her. "You make it fucking impossible to keep shit from you."

"What are you talking about?"

I shook my head. "I left out part of what Lauren just told me. I didn't want to upset you."

"What did she say?"

I took a deep breath. "Lauren's seven weeks pregnant."

Gia stared at me for a long time. I don't know how I expected her to react, but it certainly wasn't what she did next.

She started to laugh. At first lightly, but that turned into a full-fledged belly laugh. I couldn't help but join in. The entire fucking situation was just ludicrous. This shit was better than a *Jerry Springer* episode. We laughed so hard that Gia snorted and said she had to pee. Then we laughed harder.

But the sad part was…we were laughing at exactly what had happened to my mother and Elliott's mother—twenty-eight years ago.

Round two, here we come.

———

"You made the right decision." Gia rested her hand on my bouncing leg to settle it. "The doctors are going to come through those doors anytime now and tell us that he's fine."

After we spoke to the doctors last night, I signed the consent forms for Edward's surgery. We slept a few hours at the nearby Hilton again and then came back this morning in time to send him off for his operation. They'd wheeled him in about four hours ago, saying it should take about three and a half. Gia assumed what I'd been distracted and freaked out about was Edward, which was only partially true.

Even though Gia and I had a good laugh over the insanity of Lauren being pregnant, it brought a lot of bad memories back to the forefront of my mind. Lauren's kid would be like Elliott growing up…the heir apparent. Gia's would be like me in this awful family dynamic of having a father who didn't give a flying fuck about his bastard child. I didn't think I could handle another lifetime of shit that came along with being intertwined with that family. Of course, this new shit had to rear its ugly head just as I was easing my way back to Gia—thinking it could work for us. But doubt crept back in again now. And it made me fucking miserable. Because time was running out, and I knew I needed to either end this with Gia and let her move on, or get the fuck over myself.

A voice called my name and snapped me out of my thoughts. "Mr. Rushmore?"

Gia and I stood as the doctor who performed Edward's surgery walked over.

He pulled the paper mask from his mouth and slipped the blue matching hat from his head. "Good news. Your father did great. We were able to remove the aneurysm and repair the artery wall without too much bleeding."

"That's great," I said. I didn't want to care, but at the same time, I couldn't help feeling relieved that he pulled through.

"He's got a very long road to recovery." The doctor put a hand on my shoulder. "But I'm optimistic he'll make it there. It won't be easy. Your father's going to need you now, more than ever."

I was just about to thank him when a voice from behind me cut me off. A drunk, slurring, evil voice.

"No one ever needed you."

CHAPTER 20

Gia

Rookie move. *You never grab the arm of a guy in a fight.* That part I remembered. Yet I couldn't for the life of me recall what Rush had said you *should* do when you break up a fight. He'd told me something after I stupidly got in the middle of that rooftop brawl at The Heights months ago. Rush and Elliott were nose to nose since the doctor left the waiting room, and I was pretty sure things were about to get ugly.

"Rush," I said. He didn't even hear me.

"Get the fuck out of here. We don't need you hanging around." Elliott slurred his words.

Rush spoke between clenched teeth. "Yeah? Someone has to act like a man and stick around to make decisions. By the way, your father had a fatal aneurysm in his stomach. He had it removed today and lived through it. You're welcome."

"You aren't a man. You're a street thug." Elliott had been swaying back and forth and started to tip forward. Rush had to put his hand up to keep him from falling into him while he spoke.

"Sit your ass down!" Rush roared. I immediately planted my ass on the chair next to me, even though he hadn't been speaking to me. I'd never heard him so angry. Unfortunately, drunk Elliott didn't scare as easily as me. Watching the two of them insult each other nose to nose, I felt like I was sitting waiting for something bad to happen, which I realized was stupid. I might not remember what Rush had said should be done to break up a fight, but I was clear on the fact that I was supposed to call Oak. Since he wasn't around, I decided to get some assistance stopping this disaster waiting to happen, rather than dealing with the fallout afterward.

Rush and Elliott were so focused on each other, I was able to slip out of the waiting room without an argument. Lucky for me, I found a burly security guard right down the hall. After explaining to him about the tense situation, he followed me back to the waiting room.

The uniformed guard walked up to the stare off that was still going on. "Everything okay in here, boys?"

"Fine," Rush answered without averting his eyes from Elliott.

"It's not looking too fine. Having a loved one in the ICU can be stressful and can cause a lot of friction when it comes to deciding on care. But this isn't how things get handled here. I'm going to have to ask you both to take a seat, or I'll escort you both off hospital grounds."

After a solid fifteen seconds of more intense staring, it was Rush who took the high road. He shook his head, turned around, and took a seat.

Elliott started to snicker like he'd won something. So the guard took Rush's place and folded his arms across his chest while standing toe to toe. "Your turn. Sit down."

The drunk idiot mumbled under his breath, but finally went to sit on the other side of the room.

The guard looked over at me, then at Rush. "I'm going to stick around for a while. Just gonna take a seat near the door."

I smiled. "Thank you."

Rush sat alone stewing and didn't acknowledge the guard or me. I knew that, for him, Elliott's presence was a painful reminder that I was pregnant with his brother's child and the mountain of animosity it would cause for years to come. No doubt it also stirred up his own childhood hard feelings that he'd done his best to move past. It was my fault that everything was again such a mess.

I had a doctor's appointment this afternoon that I'd planned to cancel. But I started to think things might be better if I wasn't here. My presence was gasoline on an already hot fire. Rush needed to be here for the sake of his father, and I didn't need to add to his problems. So I decided to text my dad and see if he might be off today and could run me back out east for my appointment.

Two minutes later, he responded *no problem* and that he was out running errands and would swing by the hospital when he was done. I figured I'd let Rush know after he cooled off a bit.

A half-hour later, Elliott was snoring in a chair and Rush still hadn't looked up. He was taking longer to cool down than I'd thought. I stood.

"I'm going to go find a ladies' room. Want me to get you some coffee or something while I'm gone?"

Rush shook his head.

Okay, then.

I took my time in the ladies' room. Since it was a one-person restroom, I decided to wash up in the sink in case I didn't have time to stop home before my doctor's appointment. Being in the hospital made me paranoid about germs, and I'd been sweating over the Rush and Elliott standoff.

I washed my face and hands, then stripped out of my shirt and washed under my arms. Before I slipped my top back on, I took a good look in the mirror. My stomach was much rounder these days. It wouldn't be long before I moved out of the *did she gain a little weight* phase and into the *oh she got herself knocked up* phase. It had been a while since I'd had a talk with the little guy, and as odd of a time and place as it was to have one right now, it felt like it was needed.

I rubbed my belly. "Hey. It's me. Mom." Saying the word *Mom* was so foreign to me since I didn't have one of my own growing up. The word didn't roll off my tongue like it did for most people. "Sorry I haven't talked to you in a while. I've had a lot going on. That's no excuse; I know. But I'll try not to have such large gaps of time between our talks. You're getting so big. Well, at least *I'm* getting big. So I hope you're the cause of it. Although, let's be honest, I've spent a lot of time with my buddies Ben & Jerry lately. Today we're going to the doctor for a checkup. Your grandpa Tony is taking us. He's pretty awesome. The best dad anyone could ask for. I have no doubt that he's going to be an even better grandpa to you. He's kind and loving and the most dependable person on this planet. We're lucky to have him." I paused for a few seconds. "Okay. Well, that's it for now. But I'll catch up with you again real soon."

After I got dressed, I felt better about going back to the waiting room. Only when I walked in, there were three men now waiting—a sleeping Elliott, and my dad and Rush standing and talking.

Rush's eyes pinned me the minute I approached. "You didn't mention your dad was coming."

"I…uh…I have a doctor's appointment this afternoon."

The muscle in his jaw ticked. "I would have taken you."

"I know you would've. But you need to stay here. And my dad was off today."

"Taking care of you takes priority over everything else," Rush said. He was clearly not happy that I hadn't discussed it with him.

"Thank you. I know that."

My father reached out his hand. "Call me if there is anything at all I can do, son. Even if you just want some company while you're waiting here. I can always swing over on my break or go off the clock for a little while."

"Thanks, Tony. I appreciate that."

I stepped forward and gave Rush a hug. Even though he put an arm around me, his body was stiff. "Text me later," I said. "Let me know how Edward's doing."

Rush nodded.

My dad opened the door for me, and I started to walk through, but then stopped and looked back over my shoulder. Rush looked up and our eyes met, but he didn't say anything or try to stop me from leaving—not that I'd expected him to. But it was a sad reality check. This was what it was going to be like next week: me leaving with Dad, only I'd be leaving the Hamptons then. And when I said goodbye to Rush, it would be permanent.

———

I started to drag by eight o'clock. The Heights was busy, and it was a struggle to keep up. Although I perked up about ten minutes ago when Rush finally walked in. He looked haggard, still in the same clothes he wore when we'd left for the City yesterday. I assumed he had spent the rest of the day at the hospital and come directly to work. I'd texted him earlier in the day to let him know everything went okay at my doctor's appointment and asked how things were going at the hospital. His response was short. 'Haven't killed the asshole yet. So that's a plus.'

It took until almost nine-thirty for the dinner rush to have a lull long enough for me to pop into the boss's office. I knocked on the open door. "Hey. How are you?"

"Holding up. You?"

"I'm good."

"No fight with Elliott?"

"No, but he did get a black eye."

"How?"

"The asshole fell off the chair he was passed out on in the waiting room. Landed right on his face. It was the highlight of my day."

I smiled. "How's Edward?"

"Doctors said he's doing really well. They're going to try to bring him out of the coma in a few days."

"That's great."

Rush nodded and picked up a pile of papers. He turned to dump them in the file cabinet behind him while speaking. "How was your day with your dad?"

"It was good, actually. Since we had a little time, we stopped by my apartment so he could help me move around some furniture. I've been ordering stuff for the baby and needed to make some room."

Rush froze. He stayed with his back to me for a minute before turning around. When he did, he leveled me with an intense stare. "So I guess you're all set, then. To move back."

I looked down. "Yeah. I'm getting there."

When I looked up, Rush was still glaring at me. "I'm happy for you." He grabbed a file from his desk and spoke while looking at it. "Did you need anything else? I have a lot of work to catch up on."

"Oh. No. I'll let you get back to it, then."

Somehow, I managed to put one foot in front of the other and shut Rush's office door behind me. But I wasn't sure how I was ever going to put the man behind me when I walked out that door next week.

CHAPTER 21

Rush

I was tired.

Damn tired.

Between trekking back and forth from the hospital to the Hamptons and Gia's looming departure, my head was just constantly spinning.

My father was finally taken out of his coma, which was a relief. It was still going to be a long road to recovery, one that wasn't made any easier by Elliott's asinine behavior lately. Not that he wasn't always an ass, but he'd taken it to a whole new level in recent months. It seemed like he was going off the deep end.

Driving home from the City, I had to curb the urge to pull over and buy cigarettes about a dozen times. Every time I wanted to stop, I'd force myself to think about this commercial that used to come on when I was a kid. It had always scared the shit out of me. The man on the screen spoke with a hole in his throat, warning against smoking. Then, at the end, you'd see the guy had died. So I would force myself to think about that commercial every time I almost gave in. It seemed to be working. I'd gone this long without caving. Hopefully, I could keep it up.

It was late and pitch black out. The lights on the highway looked like a bunch of blurry, illuminated lines. I blinked several times to see straight.

I'd just gotten off the Long Island Expressway when the headlights of an oncoming car came into focus. Suddenly, it seemed like the car was headed straight toward me.

Shit!

Gia.

I swerved, nearly losing control of my Mustang. And then it was over.

Gia.

What just happened?

Did I almost just get hit head-on?

My heart was practically exploding out of my chest. My body was shaking.

Gia.

It was still unclear to me whether the car was headed into mine, whether I was the one at fault, or whether I'd just overreacted. All I knew was that for a split second, I felt like I was going to die. And in that moment, it was Gia I thought about.

Well, isn't that an eye opener.

Keeping my speed down, I wiped my forehead with my sleeve and continued to drive while trying to grab my bearings.

Everything on the radio was pissing me off as I kept flying through the stations, giving each song a two-second opportunity to win me over before rejection.

Nope.

Nope.

Nope.

I finally shut it off.

My phone started ringing. Glancing down, I saw that it was my mother.

With my heart still thundering against my chest, I answered, "Hey, Ma."

The television seemed to be on in the background as she said, "You sound out of breath."

I exhaled. "Yeah."

"I had a strange feeling that something was wrong," she said. "So I decided to call you and check in. Are you okay?"

Chills ran through me. She had a strange feeling? If that wasn't creepy, I didn't know what was. This night just kept getting weirder.

"You freaked me out just now," I said.

"What do you mean?"

"When you said you sensed something. Because I'm pretty sure I might have almost died. Either that, or I'm losing my mind."

"What?" She sounded panicked. "What happened?"

"I'm fine. I didn't mean to scare you, but I just averted a head-on collision. At least, I think I did. It happened so fast, I'm not sure if I overreacted, or if I was really in danger of getting hit. Nothing like that has ever happened to me. All I know is…I'm sweating like a motherfucker right now. Excuse my language."

"Thank God you're okay. You've been under too much stress."

"I've always worked well under pressure. Not sure why all of a sudden it's catching up with me."

"Well, you just answered your own question. Everyone has a breaking point. You're allowed for once in your life to lose it a little, son. But please be careful, and try not to drive when you're tired if you can help it. I hope you learned your lesson."

"You want to know the kicker? As this car was supposedly careening toward me, all I could think about was Gia."

"Oh, Heath, what does that tell you?"

I sighed into the phone. "I know what I feel. I just don't know if that's enough."

"The right decision will come to you, Heath. But you need to take care of yourself before you can think with a clear mind. It's okay to be worrying about everyone else, but at some point you have to take care of your health, too. Look at what you've been through in just a matter of months. You fell in love for the first time in your life, found out she was pregnant, then found out the unimaginable about who the father of the baby is. Not to mention, the only real father figure in your life passed away, and your *actual* father was near death."

Damn, when she put it like that, it sounded crazy as fuck. "Thanks for the reminder, Ma. Now I need a cigarette *and* a drink."

Once I arrived back at my place, the reality of what might have almost happened tonight hit me. I could have died. Then what? Who would look after Gia? That was a screwed-up thought to have when I hadn't fully committed to her—to them. A part of me knew that even if I couldn't go through with being a father to Elliott's child, that I was going to protect them somehow, even if from afar. She felt like she needed to prepare for a life apart from me, but I would find a way to take care of them no matter what.

But what happens when she finds somebody else?

Because she *will* find somebody else. You gonna take care of her while she's with someone? How does that make sense?

Fucking some other guy?

The mere thought of that scenario made me ill beyond comprehension.

I threw my keys down and opened my fridge. Nothing seemed appealing. Opening the freezer, I spotted an old carton of Ben & Jerry's Chunky Monkey that had been left over from the last time Gia was here. That seemed like ages ago.

Might as well finish it off.

When I opened up the carton, there was a sticky note attached to the underside of the top.

There's not much left. I'm sorry. Got a late night craving. I'll replace it. I love you.

She never had a chance to replace it, because she hadn't been here since. Now my chest hurt. I didn't want to touch the damn ice cream anymore. All I wanted to do now was go to sleep and shut off my thoughts for a while.

I headed upstairs to my bedroom and opened the French doors that led out to the balcony. Letting the cool evening breeze into my room, I lay back and listened to the sounds of the waves while I inhaled the salty air. This was the best part of living where I did. The ocean had a calming effect on me like nothing else did.

And I knew just what I was going to do to seal the deal on falling asleep. There was only one way I was going to be able to relax enough to do that.

I had three photos in a hidden album in my phone that always did the trick when I wanted to come fast. The images were of Gia during the last week we were together before the Elliott news surfaced. Totally naked and spread eagle, she was taunting me in the pic, inviting me to claim her. It was the perfect shot, because you could see everything, including her gorgeous tits. That night, I had asked if I could snap some naked shots of her and she'd said yes. At the time, I had no idea that those photos would become a replacement for the real thing. Looking at them now was a form of self-torture, one I couldn't seem to resist from time to time.

Just as I'd unzipped my pants and taken my rock hard dick out, the photo of Gia's pussy began to vibrate in my hand.

Gia calling.

I laughed at the irony. Fitting.

Sorry, Gia. I can't talk right now. Your pussy is calling to me instead.

Sexually frustrated, I picked up. "Hey."

"Hi…I just wanted to check in on you and find out how Edward is doing."

"No difference since they took him out of the coma. He's stable. Thank you for checking." I opted not to tell her about my near-death experience, mainly because I didn't want to stress her out even more in her condition.

"What are you up to tonight?" she asked.

Uh.

I couldn't help but laugh. My eyes were watering.

"What's so funny?"

"Your pussy just vibrated."

She gasped. "Wait…how did you know that?"

Huh?

Her bizarre question made me laugh again. I knew what I was referring to. But what the hell was *she* referring to?

"Hold up…your pussy is actually vibrating?" I asked.

"Yes. But how did you know?"

I started to crack up even harder. "What in God's name are you talking about, Gia?"

"What are *you* talking about?" she asked, sounding confused. "I thought we were talking about the same thing. I just don't know how you would even know about that."

"You need to go first. Explain to me what you're talking about."

She sighed. "Well, I've been getting this strange sensation down there. It feels like vibrations—like the faint feeling of a cell phone going off inside my vagina. But very faint. I actually called my doctor about it. He thinks it's hormonal or maybe some type of muscle fasciculation from stress. Like the same kind of thing that happens when you're nervous or have too much caffeine."

"Muscle what?"

"Fasciculation. Like a muscle twitch."

"Ah, yeah…I get those in my dick," I snickered.

"Shut up." She was laughing now, too. "But the question is…how on Earth did you know?"

This conversation was seriously up there with one of the strangest I'd ever had.

Wiping my eyes, I said, "I didn't, Gia. I didn't know about your vibrating pussy." I snorted.

"But you brought it up!"

"I was referring to my *own* vibrating pussy—or rather your pussy vibrating in my hand."

"What? I'm so confused."

"Okay…you interrupted something when you called."

"Something?"

"Yeah, I was just about to jack off."

"Oh…gotcha."

"To pictures of you, if you must know. I was using a photo of your naked pussy to get off. Remember the pictures I took of you a while back?"

"Yeah, uh-huh."

"When you called, the phone started vibrating. Thus… vibrating pussy."

She laughed. "Wow. Okay. Now it all makes total sense… but that's really coincidental. You know I can help you out, I'm just a phone call away, and maybe you could even help me with my own vibrating pussy."

"Gia…"

It took everything in me not to jump in my car and take all of my frustrations out on her. But I wasn't thinking straight tonight. It was safer for me to just stay here in my bed where I couldn't crash into cars or violate a vibrating pussy.

CHAPTER 22

Gia

Riley stood near the door of my bedroom. "I can't believe you're leaving this week, too." She crossed her arms. "I was sure everything was going to work out with you guys. I still have faith, though."

Riley was watching me get dressed for the end-of-the-season party at The Heights. Given that she knew nothing about Elliott being the father of my baby, it was no surprise that she was utterly confused about why I had to leave.

"This has been a wild summer. I'll never forget it," she said.

"Neither will I."

"Do you think you'll come back next summer?"

Was she serious?

"With the baby? No. My life as I know it is pretty much over, Riley. No more summer shares for about eighteen years."

She blew out a breath. "It's just hard to believe that things won't ever be the same again."

Her words hit me hard. In her mind, I was certain she was referring to no more "fun in the sun." For me, they meant so much more. Whether or not Rush ever came around, things would never be the same for us. Either he would be gone from my life, or we would have to adjust to a whole new set of challenges. I just wished he loved me enough to want to fight for the latter, even if it was painful. But I didn't get to choose how this was going to play out.

"What do you plan on doing when you get to the City?" she asked.

"Well, I have to find a job. That's number one. And I have to finish my book. That's number two. Hopefully, once I'm there, I'll be able to focus more on the writing."

"I can't wait to read this book when it's done. I don't even read romance, but I'll read this one." Her eyes widened. "Hey…you should put Rush on the cover. Bet that would sell."

For some reason, that rubbed me the wrong way. Maybe that's just because I was extra sensitive, but I really didn't want to hear another woman pointing out how attractive my likely soon-to-be ex was.

"I can't really see him posing. He's not really the Fabio type."

"Well, that's definitely true." She laughed.

Riley went downstairs, leaving me alone with my thoughts. I'd picked the prettiest maternity dress I owned to wear to the party tonight. It was black and gold with a sequined neckline. It was cut in a way that hid my ever-protruding stomach.

I was absolutely dreading having to say goodbye to Rush soon. The quicker the exit, the better. No long goodbyes for me. I just couldn't handle it.

Everything was packed away except for the last few items that I kept in my room because I needed the strength they gave me.

I grabbed them one by one as I prepared to take them with me.

Melody's sunset painting. While it made me sad, it also gave me hope and helped remind me that this summer was a magical journey, despite the painful parts. The sun always sets and rises, no matter what. Tomorrow is always a new day. This painting would continue to give me hope for years to come.

The black-haired doll that Rush bought me from the thrift store. While I had packed all of my other ugly dolls away, I just hadn't been able to part with that one yet. It was a reminder of just how much Rush really "got me" and how even in the worst of times, he always knew how to make me smile.

Rush's black shirt—the one I wore as a dress to Elliott's party, the night I discovered he was Harlan. That shirt was my reality check. It reminded me not to let my guard down whenever I would start to believe that love trumped all. It was a protective mechanism, one I wouldn't be returning to its rightful owner, especially since after all this time, it still smelled like him.

I started to break down as I packed the shirt away. Elliott still didn't know about the baby. I could only imagine how terrible telling him was going to be. My biggest fear was that he would try to capitalize on it in some way, namely hurting me to get to Rush.

The hyped-up end-of-the-season party definitely lived up to its reputation.

Rush had gone all out tonight. There were huge lanterns set up outside. A local cover band that was really hard to get was playing on the rooftop. He'd booked them a year in advance for this event. The weather was absolutely gorgeous with a light breeze and perfect for the outdoor bar.

We were full to capacity. I sort of floated through the party, refusing to actually think about what this night meant. I couldn't allow myself to dwell on it long enough to cry.

The evening was just passing on by, but I really wished it would slow down. Rush was nowhere to be found. I couldn't tell if he was just tending to things or hiding from me. But I definitely felt his absence tonight, not only on the floor but in my heart.

The sooner you get used to it, the better.

Oak came around a corner. "How you holding up, pretty lady?"

Just the sight of Oak made me sad. He'd been such a good friend and advocate. I was really going to miss seeing him all the time. A giant man with a giant heart.

"Hey…before I forget to tell you…" I said. "Thank you for everything this summer…for looking out for me here and for your support through the worst of everything. I'll never forget it."

"Whoa. That sounds an awful lot like goodbye."

I shrugged. "Well, it sort of is. It's our last night of work. Just a few more days, and I'll be back in Queens."

Oak looked like he was at a loss for words. Then he finally said, "I refuse to believe Rush is gonna let you go, Gia. I refuse to believe I won't be seeing you anymore."

"He's made no effort to stop me." I looked around the crowded room and my voice cracked. "I haven't even seen him all night. Have you?"

"He's around, yeah. He's probably struggling in his own way with the same thing you are."

A wave of sadness hit me. At that moment, I saw Rush's mom, Melody, walk in.

Great. There was no way I was going to be able to hide my tears now.

She headed straight toward me.

I tried to act happy as I hugged her. "Melody, I wasn't sure if you'd be here."

"I never miss this party, and tomorrow's the employee brunch, but I certainly couldn't miss any of it knowing that you're leaving soon."

"Rush and I…we aren't…"

She smiled sympathetically and reached for my hand. "I know, sweetheart. I know."

"I haven't seen him around much tonight," I told her.

Melody didn't seem surprised. "That's probably intentional."

"That's what I was afraid of."

"I wouldn't take that to mean he doesn't care…just the opposite, Gia. Pretty sure this is one of the hardest nights of his life. He's probably avoiding you to keep from getting upset. He won't be able to hide all night, though."

Hearing her say that made me want to go find him.

Things were busy, and I was standing around ignoring customers. "I have to get back to work. Will you make some time for me after closing?"

Melody placed her hand on my arm. "Of course. That's why I'm here. Spending the night at Rush's tonight."

"Okay." I smiled.

Melody went to mingle, and I resumed my duties, seating people and flashing fake smiles to customers.

It wasn't until about an hour later that Rush finally appeared. I swore I felt his presence before I even noticed him standing there. Something in the room just shifted. Then I turned and there he was.

He took my breath away. Rush was more dressed up than usual, wearing a black polo that showcased his tatted arms and pants that hugged his beautiful ass. Damn, he looked amazing.

I guess I assumed he would continue to ignore me. But he did the last thing I expected. He came over to me and grabbed my hand. He was leading me outside.

My heart started to pound. "What are you doing? I have to finish up my shift."

"I've got it covered. You're off for the rest of the night."

"I am?"

"Yes."

It felt so good to be holding his hand. It had been too long. He led me out the door and all the way down to the water, then sat down on the sand and patted the ground, prompting me to situate myself between his legs. Rush enveloped me in his arms and placed his cheek on my back.

My entire body seemed to calm down instantly. He was quiet, and I relished the heat of his body against mine as we sat there together.

I didn't understand what was happening, and I didn't question it. In my mind, silence was good. It meant he couldn't tell me that whatever this was between us now was over. As far as I was concerned, silence bought us more time.

Finally, I had to ask, "What are we doing?"

Yes, that question was both literal and figurative.

"Nothing. Absolutely nothing. We're just sitting. I want to enjoy this moment with you out here. Is that okay?"

"Yeah. I'm just surprised. You were ignoring me all night."

"You really think you were far from my mind, Gia?"

I didn't answer because it was a rhetorical question. Of course, I was on his mind.

He continued, "You're all I can think about tonight. Hell, any night."

We were silent again for a long while. It felt damn good to be in his arms again, a feeling of safety like no other. I looked back at The Heights in the distance, and all of the chaos of the party seemed like a distant memory compared to our peaceful retreat.

He spoke against my back. "I'm sorry I was MIA tonight. It was hard for me to deal with it being your last night at The Heights. It was easier for me not to deal with it at all."

"It's okay. I get it. I know it's hard. We're both in this together. It's hard for me, too."

He spoke against my back. "When I finally came to the main dining room, I looked over at you, and immediately regretted wasting the whole night ruminating in my office when I could have spent it looking at you in this dress. You look so beautiful."

I turned my head around and just couldn't help it, giving him a gentle kiss on the lips. "I'm glad you stole me away."

He ran his hand through my hair. "You're coming to the staff brunch tomorrow afternoon, right?"

"Yeah…I'll be there but I have some more packing to do in the morning."

He didn't respond to that.

I continued sitting between his legs staring out at the ocean, wondering if I would ever see this body of water again. If things didn't work out, would I ever come back, or would it simply be too painful?

Rush placed both of his hands on my belly and began to rub. I closed my eyes. It felt so good. There wasn't any better feeling than a man with big, beautiful hands rubbing your stomach. Well, maybe there were a couple of better feelings. But right now, this was just what the doctor ordered.

I felt the baby start to kick and jumped. "Did you feel that?" It wasn't the first time, but it was definitely one of the most intense.

"Yeah." He laughed. "Yeah, I did. He must like the beach."

"I think he's responding to being rubbed, actually."

"He can feel it when I do this?"

"Yes. I read that they can. Isn't that crazy?"

"Wow." He continued massaging me. "Hey, are you gonna find out what it is…a boy or a girl?"

"Why do you even need to ask if you're so sure it's a boy?" I chided.

"I want to be able to tell you I told you so."

"Actually, I think I want to be surprised. There aren't that many times in life you can choose to be surprised. I think I'd like to wait."

"Fair enough. We've definitely had enough surprises we couldn't control."

"That's for damn sure," I said.

I was practically falling asleep as he continued to rub my stomach. The baby had stopped moving, though. Maybe he fell asleep. *He.* I laughed, realizing Rush had me believing it was a boy, too.

I still couldn't believe Rush abandoned his own bar's party to spend this private time with me. This would be something I would never forget.

Suddenly, he said, "Did you feel that?"

I jumped a little. "What?"

"That."

"No? The baby moved? I didn't feel it."

"No. It's coming from here." He slid his hand below my stomach. "I think it's your pussy vibrating."

I giggled and elbowed him in the side. "Jerk."

CHAPTER 23

Rush

Normally, I couldn't wait for the summer season to be over. I'd be fed up with snobby customers, unreliable staff who call in sick for a damn sunburn, and ready for the stop-and-go tourists to get the hell off the road. But not this year. This year, I wasn't ready to see it end. And the reason for that was currently walking around hugging all the staff with tears in her eyes.

I walked over as she hugged Oak. It was the second one she'd given him, and a pang of jealousy might've crept in, no matter how ludicrous I knew it was.

"You do realize that you're going to see everyone at the Morning After brunch tomorrow, right?"

She sniffled back tears. "I know. But this is the last night that we'll all be working together."

"So does that mean tonight you cry because you're done working with these people and then tomorrow you cry all over again because you'll *actually* be saying goodbye?"

Gia stuck out her tongue. "Shut up."

I smirked. "What'd I tell you about sticking out that tongue at me, little girl?"

Oak shook his head and chuckled. It was almost five in the morning, the last of the customers were booted out an hour ago, and most of my staff had left, with the exception of Riley, Oak, Gia, and one of the busboys. They all walked to the front door at once.

I unlocked it to let them out. "See you at two tomorrow?"

Oak shook my hand and everyone but Gia piled out. She stood on her tippy toes and kissed my cheek. "Good night, Heathcliff."

"Get some sleep, sweetheart."

After I watched them all get into their cars and safely take off, I locked the door. I needed to get some sleep myself. The Morning After party was a tradition I started when I took over The Heights. The day after the year-end bash, I threw a brunch for all of my employees. I did the setup, serving, and pouring—which the employees all seemed to get a kick out of every year. But that meant that I needed to be back here pretty early in order to make sure everything was ready when they arrived.

Yet I didn't feel like leaving still. So I shut off all the lights, took a tablecloth from the supply closet to lie down on, and headed out back to the beach. It was still dark, but it wouldn't be too long before the sun started to come up. Normally I was a sunset kind of guy—sitting around reflecting on my day and watching Mother Nature put the sky to bed. I liked a fade-to-black ending. It had always seemed fitting for my life. But today sunrise seemed right—the dawn of a new day bringing hope and a chance to start over fresh. Maybe it would shed some figurative light on me while the literal took over the sky.

"Hey, Rush." Oak's wife Min walked over and gave me a hug while holding one of her and Oak's daughters on her hip. Every time I saw Min Lee, I got a kick out of how tiny she was. She couldn't be more than five foot tall and weigh a hundred pounds soaking wet. If I didn't think he'd clock me, I'd be busting her husband's balls about how the hell they made that shit work in the sack.

"Hey, Min. You look great. Still don't understand what you see in that big doofus." I winked.

"Watch it," Oak said. "There's no bouncer on duty right now to save your scrawny ass if I decide to use your head as a punching bag."

Only a dude as enormous as Oak could call a guy my size scrawny. I chuckled. "You don't scare me," I joked while pulling his wife in front of me like a human shield.

"That's right. Put the person with the biggest cajones in front of you for protection."

We all laughed. While Oak and his family settled in, I went and got them their drinks: a mimosa for Min and a beer for my buddy. We liked to argue and screw around, but I had needed Oak a lot this year. He'd been my confidant with everything going on with Gia, and it would have sucked without him. That's why I'd stuck an extra two grand in his end-of-year bonus this year. He deserved it just for putting up with my whining ass.

The rest of the staff and their families trickled in. I played hostess with the mostest, handing out bonus checks with an endless flow of drinks. Gia walked in late with her dad. I hadn't realized that he was coming out from Queens for the party.

I shook his hand. "Hey, Tony. Nice to see you."

"You, too, son. You must be glad the busy season is over."

My eyes flashed to Gia and back. "It's bittersweet."

Gia had been looking down, seemingly lost in thought. And she looked nervous for some reason. When I touched her shoulder to lean in and kiss her cheek hello, she jumped.

"What's going on? You okay?" I asked.

"Yeah. I'm fine. Just tired."

I nodded, but would definitely be keeping an eye on her.

Once everyone had full plates and drinks, I went to the bar to make a few more batches of mimosas. Tony walked over and took a seat on a stool across from me. He looked over his shoulder at Gia before starting to talk. She was busy yapping with my mother.

"I take it from the surprise on your face when I walked in that you didn't know that I would be here."

I set down the container of orange juice in my hand. "I didn't. But I'm glad you're here. This party is for family, and I'm glad Gia invited you."

Tony nodded. "I'm also guessing that you don't know why I'm here?"

"Is everything okay with Gia?"

"Physically, yes. She's fine. But when did she tell you she was moving back to Queens?"

"Her lease is up on Friday, so in a few days."

Tony shook his head back and forth slowly. "She called me last night. Moved that up."

My entire body went rigid. "To when?"

"Right after this party. Said she wanted to get a jump on settling back in. But my gut told me she might be trying to sneak out without saying goodbye to a certain boss. I drove out early this morning and loaded almost everything already. Just need to move a few more boxes, and we'll be pulling out."

Fuck.

Fuck.

Fuck!

I stared down at the bar. After a while, I looked up at Tony but wasn't in any condition to talk to anyone. "I need to step outside for a bit."

He nodded. "Go ahead, son. I'll finish making the drinks and tell anyone who looks for you that you needed to take a call."

I slipped out back and started to walk on the beach. Inside my chest, I had a crushing sensation that I hoped might be a heart attack. Gia wouldn't fucking leave me if I was in ICU. Then again, is that really what it would take to get her to stay? I was pretty sure that it could be a hell of a lot easier than that. All I needed to do was tell her I wanted to be with her. Tell her I could accept her child and move on without spending every day loathing the thought of her baby's father. Tell her I could move on without resentment. Why couldn't I do it? I *wanted* to fucking do it.

I had to sit down on a big rock when I started to hyperventilate. My head was spinning, and I started to think maybe the lack of sleep and stress really had induced a heart attack. It took a solid ten minutes of sitting with my head between my legs, taking measured breaths in order for the pain to subside.

Afraid people might start to leave because I was gone so long, I started to walk back. I hadn't been wrong. People were milling around and beginning to say goodbye to one another.

Riley came up to me first. "Thanks for everything this season, Rush. You're not as big of an asshole boss as I originally thought."

Somehow I managed to fake a smile and say goodbye on autopilot to most of the staff. I wouldn't remember anything any of them said later because my brain was entirely somewhere else, but at least no one seemed to notice.

At one point, I found myself staring at Oak and his oldest daughter. She had to be about eight or nine now, and was showing off some dance routine to one of the female bartenders. It wasn't his daughter who had caught my attention, but rather the way Oak was looking at her while she twirled around. So much love and adoration in his eyes. Sensing someone watching him, he looked up and our eyes caught. He smiled and patted his chest as if to tell me—*this is life, man.* I had to swallow a few times.

Gia made her way over to me, her dad standing a few feet behind her watching our interaction. When she had arrived earlier, I'd suspected she was nervous, but now it was glaringly obvious. She wrung her hands and looked anywhere but in my eyes. "So…I'll give you a call tomorrow."

I stared at her. "You're not leaving until Friday, right?"

Her guilt-filled eyes flashed up to mine before darting away again. "Yep. Friday."

Tony shook his head from behind her and frowned.

So this was it? This was how it would go down? Like a goddamned pussy, I was going to let the woman I loved lie to me and sneak off.

"Gia…I…"

Her eyes came back to mine. They were filled with hope and optimism. But instead of giving me strength, they reminded me that I couldn't hurt her again. Looking down, I said. "Nothing. I was just going to ask if I'd given you your check, but then I remembered that I did."

"Oh. Okay."

She stepped forward and gave me a hug that I could barely reciprocate. I had no balls left. In the end, I couldn't even make it easier for her and be the one to walk away. She had to be the one to do it. In that moment, I felt ashamed to be a man.

Gia quickly turned away, and I got the feeling it might be to hide tears. Tony stepped forward and shook my hand as she walked to the door. "We'll be around for another hour or two—in case you think of anything last minute you might need to talk to Gia about."

I sat in the middle of the restaurant floor alone. Everyone had left, including Gia and her lie. Looking around, I realized that I felt a lot like the restaurant right now—alone and empty.

I closed my eyes and started to think about my life.

The women—I couldn't even remember any of the faces. Except Gia's.

My father—I'd spent my life trying to prove to everyone that I didn't give a shit about the man, yet all I ever really wanted was for him to want me.

My mother—Everything she'd sacrificed to raise me on her own.

Elliott—Most people wouldn't believe me if I said I was jealous of him. But I was. From the time we were little, he had what I wanted, even if I would never admit it—love and acceptance from our father. And now he even had what I wanted more than anything in the world—to be the father of Gia's baby. Life could be so damn cruel sometimes.

Pat—The father figure I had growing up who died way too early. How much he had meant to me growing up.

Gia—*My beautiful Gia.*

I loved her more than I thought I could handle. Yet here I sat letting the best thing that ever happened to me walk out the door. I fucking hated myself for it. I just wished there was some way to be sure that I could handle everything coming our way, that I wouldn't resent her and the baby because of the constant reminder of my own childhood and the identity of the baby's biological father.

Exhausted and feeling like I might not even be able to drive home soon, I went to my office to lock the safe before heading home. The lights were off, but sunlight shined through the partially covered window allowing me to see well enough, so I didn't bother to flip on the switch as I entered. Unfortunately, it hadn't been bright enough for me to see that one of the wheels had come off the bottom of my chair, and I almost cracked my head on the corner of the desk when I fell off of it. On my way down, I'd reached to grab onto something and knocked a stack of files off my desk, unleashing a torrent of papers that landed on top of me. *Perfect, just fucking perfect.*

Picking them up, I tossed them back on the desk and an envelope fell out from one of the files. I didn't recognize it, but the handwriting was familiar and stopped me. *Gia's handwriting.*

Ripping it open, I unfolded the contents and found a regular eight-and-a-half-by-eleven piece of paper with a few typewritten lines centered in the middle. There was also a yellow sticky note attached. I read that first.

I hope you like the dedication for my book. Only we'll know how our story ends and be able to fill in the next sentence.

My eyes drifted up to the words typed in the middle of the page.

> *To Rush. Fortunately, I was a horrible bartender and caught the eye of the mean owner whom I fell madly in love with...*

I had no idea when she'd stuck the envelope in my office or if she'd hoped I'd find it today or not. But I mentally started to fill in the words that came next.

Unfortunately, he was a douchebag who didn't love me enough back.

Unfortunately, he ran away when life threw us a curve ball.

Unfortunately, he never got to meet Gia's son.

That last part really fucked with my head. How could I possibly not meet her little boy? It didn't feel like *her* little boy...he felt like *our* little boy.

I reread her note again. *Only we'll know how our story ends and be able to fill in the next sentence.* Was this really how our story ended? It sure as hell didn't feel like it was over.

Unfortunately, he never got to meet Gia's son.

Fuck that. What the hell was I doing? He wasn't Elliott's kid; he was my son. Pat had taught me better than anyone that paternity may be biology, but acting like a dad is a choice. And that meant a hell of a lot more than donating some sperm. I *wanted* to be with Gia. I *wanted* that baby. I *wanted* to be a family with them. No matter how much I hated my brother, Oak was right—I loved Gia more than I could possibly hate anyone.

I started to panic. *Holy shit.* What the hell did I nearly do? Grabbing my keys, I ran out of the office and straight to the parking lot. I wasn't even sure if I locked the door to the restaurant, but it wasn't important enough to go back and check. Nothing was more important than getting to Gia.

Jumping into my car, my hand shook as I put the key into the engine. I was really going to do this. Get my girl, have a baby, and live happily ever after. Suddenly, I couldn't remember one valid reason why I had been holding out. I turned the ignition and my car started to make a choking sound, right before it sputtered out.

No fucking way. This couldn't be happening. Gia's old car was the steaming hunk of shit, not mine.

I turned the key again. It started to roar to life and then quickly sputtered out again.

On the third try, it didn't even attempt to start.

Click-click.

Click-click.

The fucking car was dead.

I banged my head against the wheel a few times before taking out my phone to call Gia and make sure she didn't leave.

Her phone went to voicemail.

Fuck!

I had Tony's number from when she'd been in the hospital. Scrolling, I tried him next.

Straight to voicemail.

Fuck!

There wasn't time to call an Uber and wait. So I got out of the car and started to run. It was a good two miles to her house, but what choice did I have.

Tony was loading a box into the back of his car when I raced up the driveway so winded that I could barely even talk. Bent over with my hands on my knees and panting, I held up one finger to Tony and gulped in a few mouthfuls of air.

"Need..." *Breath. Breath.* "...to talk to Gia."

Tony smiled. "I'll take a walk around the block." He nodded his head toward the house. "Doors open. She's staring at some creepy-looking new doll in her room."

I let myself in and walked to her bedroom, trying to catch my breath as I cooled down. When I got to the doorway, her back was to me. She must've heard my footsteps and assumed they belonged to her father.

"This is the last of it. I'm sorry. I know I'm going at a snail's pace. But it's just so hard to seal up the last box and know I'll probably never be back. This place really started to feel like home."

My heart physically ached. God, I'd fucked up so royally. I hoped she could even forgive me.

I cleared my throat. "Unfortunately, the mean bartender had his head stuck up his ass and nearly let the love of his life slip through his fingers."

Gia's head whipped up and around. She stared at me and clutched at her chest. "Are you really here?"

I took a few hesitant steps into her room. "I'm really here. And I'm so fucking sorry it took me this long to come."

She looked as nervous as I felt. Who could blame her with what I'd put her through? I closed the distance between us and took the ugly doll from her hand so I could hold both of hers.

"Gia. I'm not just in love with you. I'm in love with that little boy you're carrying for us, too. It doesn't matter if it wasn't my sperm that made him. It matters that I'm going to love him and treat him as my own. If you can find it in your heart to forgive me, I promise that I'll love and take care of both of you no different than if we'd made him. I want to be the man your son looks up to, no matter what the DNA says."

Tears streamed down her cheeks. "I'm afraid to believe that this is true. That you're really here and saying all this to me right now."

"I know. And that's my fault. But give me time and I'll make you realize that there's never been anything truer than what I feel for you. Just don't leave me. Give me another chance, and I promise I won't let you down again."

Gia looked at the floor. I held my breath while she seemed to be thinking it over. She didn't know it yet, but I wasn't taking no for answer. I'd steal her father's handcuffs and chain her to my bed if I had to. It would be my pleasure to spend the next few months doing nothing but feeding her, watching her belly grow, and fucking her senseless until she agreed to stay forever.

But trust and believing that someone was going to stick around meant a lot to both of us, so I hoped it didn't come to that. She needed to believe it could still work and that I could redeem myself. Every second that ticked by, it felt like my heart beat louder with anticipation. Eventually, she looked up.

"Fortunately, Gia really liked the sunsets from Rush's balcony, and her vibrating pussy has been pretty neglected, so she decided to stay."

I smiled from ear to ear, reached out and picked her up. Spinning her around, I said, "Fortunately, Rush is afflicted with incurable preggophilia so he can't wait to get his hands on that pussy."

Gia laughed. "You lost! You started your sentence with fortunately, and you were supposed to start with unfortunately!"

I slid her down my body and cupped both her cheeks. "No, babe, I didn't lose. From now on, there is no more *unfortunately* in our story."

I really hoped this kid was a boy because the thought of a guy who looked like me walking out to talk to me when my daughter was old enough to date really made me ill. Not to mention, I was walking out to square things with Tony after just finishing feeling up his fucking daughter.

He had been leaning against his car and pushed off when I approached.

"Sorry. I guess we had a lot to say to each other."

"Not a problem. Unless you tell me that my little girl is inside heartbroken and crying right now. But before you answer that, you should know my gun is in the glove compartment."

I smiled. "No. We're good. I apologize for how I've acted lately. It took me a while to pull my head out of my ass. But it won't happen again. She agreed to give me another chance, and I promise I won't screw it up this time."

"Good. I'm glad. And for what it's worth, if you hadn't struggled to come to your decision, I would have been more concerned. You're taking on a big responsibility here, and it's not something a person should take lightly."

I nodded. "Thanks for being so understanding."

"So she's going to stay out here?"

"Yeah. If it's alright with you, she's going to move in with me."

Tony deadpanned. "That's not alright with me. At all."

Seeing the freaked-out look on my face, Tony slapped my arm and started to laugh. "I'm just screwing with you."

I let out a breath. "You and your daughter have a sick sense of humor sometimes."

Tony chuckled and reached into the back of his car, pulling out a box. Handing it to me, he said, "This box has all her dolls. She made me put them in the car instead of the trailer. Actually watched me do it to make sure these twisted things didn't fly coach."

I smiled. "I'll drop it inside and then unload the trailer."

Tony raised his hand. "No need. Trailer's empty."

My brows drew down. "Where's the rest of her stuff? Her room is empty."

"Garage. Never loaded the trailer. Just moved them out of her room and stacked them in the garage when she wasn't paying attention."

"I don't get it."

Tony put his arm around my shoulder and started walking us toward the house. "Turns out, I'm a keen judge of character, son. Figured it would be easier to stick all those boxes in there rather than having to unload the trailer all over again when you finally pulled your head out of your ass."

CHAPTER 24

Gia

It still seemed surreal.

I rubbed my stomach as I looked out the window at Rush talking with my father. The baby was kicking up a storm. Maybe he or she could sense my stress. Even if this wasn't good for the baby, I just couldn't be calm right now.

The longer Rush lingered outside, the more scared I was that he might have changed his mind.

What were they talking about?

I watched as he took one box from my dad and walked it over to the house.

After they returned to the car, they shook hands. My father pulled Rush into a hug and patted him on the back. Then Dad drove off—with the trailer. *My stuff!* Why was Rush not helping my father unload my things if I wasn't going anywhere?

I started to panic. Had Rush told Dad to take my things back to the City after all? Was he already having second thoughts?

The front door slammed shut, and my heart pounded. Rush's quick footsteps matched the rhythm of my fervent heartbeat.

He stood in the doorway, and we just stared at each other for a bit. Rush looked like he was ready to attack me—in a good way. That both excited me and made me nervous because I was still confused about where things stood.

I had to know. "Why did my father just leave with all of my stuff? Did you tell him to take everything back to the City after all?"

His expression soured as he slowly approached me. "What? Did you not hear a word I said to you earlier?"

"Yes, but—"

"Did you *not* hear me say I would never let you down again?"

"Yes, of course I did, but my stuff was—"

"Doesn't matter." Rush's eyes were burning with intensity.

He placed his hand on his belt and began to remove it before throwing it to the side. He unzipped his pants and pushed his jeans down, letting them fall to the ground. My formerly vibrating pussy was now full-on throbbing at the sight of his engorged cock bobbing against his abdomen. Holy hell, I needed it inside of me.

Even if he had told me he'd changed his mind, I was pretty sure I might've had to beg him to fuck me right now regardless.

Rush pulled me into him and I felt his stiff erection against my belly. "Look at me," he demanded.

I arched my head to meet his incendiary stare.

"I'm gonna say it one more time. I will *never* let you down again. I don't care whether or not you thought your dad was driving away with your stuff. You need to trust me, no matter what. Do you understand?"

I nodded. "Yes."

"Your stuff is in the garage. Your father never even put it in the trailer."

My eyes widened in disbelief. "What?"

"The man is smarter than both of us. He knew I wouldn't be able to let you go."

My mouth hung open. Any amount of time I had to ponder my father's actions was short-lived when Rush placed his mouth at my ear. "I need your clothes off…need to be inside you. I can't wait any longer."

My nipples stiffened as I slipped my dress over my head before unsnapping my bra. My breasts tingled as they hit the cold air.

Rush dropped to his knees before placing both hands on my stomach and gently kissed the taut skin over my navel. He stopped to stare up at me, a look of torment in his eyes. "I missed it growing. I missed so much. You got so much bigger."

I ran my fingers through his hair. "It's gonna get a lot bigger than this. And you'll be here for all of it."

He closed his eyes and continued kissing me. It was so sweet, yet sensual and erotic.

As he continued kissing over my stomach, he said, "I've been dreaming of doing this. You're so fucking sexy. I can't take it…this body…"

I laughed. "You're crazy."

Rush was almost in a trance. He kissed lower and lower until I could feel his mouth over my underwear. He pulled my panties down, then began to devour me. I gasped at the feeling of his tongue lashing at my clit. It felt like it had been ages since I'd felt this sensation. The pressure was so intense that I nearly came over his mouth on the spot.

Before it got to that point, he suddenly got up. I looked down and salivated at the sight of his erection. I desperately needed him inside of me.

He looped his fingers through mine and led me over to the bed.

Rush hovered over me. "Tell me what you did to get off when I wasn't around…"

My voice trembled. "I used my vibrator."

"What did you think about when you used it?"

"I thought about you."

"Tell me exactly what you thought about…"

I'd forgotten how much he liked when I talked dirty. "I imagined you were fucking me hard while I played with my clit."

His eyes were glassy. "Where is your toy? Show me."

Ironically, that reminded me that I'd forgotten to pack away my vibrator, since I'd been using it up until last night. It was still in the nightstand. Some new tenant would have gotten an interesting surprise.

When I took out the hot pink, silicone rod, he took one look at it and said, "You must have missed me. That thing is pathetic." He smirked. "Lie back and spread your legs… show me what you did with it."

Rush watched me intently as I turned it on and began to massage myself. He took his cock out and started to stroke it while he stared down at me, mesmerized. I loved watching his hand moving back and forth over his thickness. He was so hard, and I could see the veins protruding through his shaft. The watching lasted all of a minute before he lowered himself down onto me. How I'd missed feeling the weight of his body over me. He threw the vibrator to the side before sinking into me, letting out an unintelligible sound. I screamed out in pleasure from the intensity of him filling me.

Finally.

Rush was groaning over and over, complete involuntary sounds of ecstasy as he thrust into me. He'd never been so vocal during sex as he was right now, and I was loving it. *Loving it.* All of my worries were temporarily fading away.

Wrapping my hands around the back of his head, I pushed his mouth into mine as he thrust harder, letting out all of the frustration from the weeks we spent apart.

I panted, "I wasn't sure if I would ever get to feel this again."

"I'm going to fuck you all night, Gia...not gonna stop until morning or until you tell me to, whichever comes first."

I clenched my muscles around him. "Harder. I can take it," I begged. "Please."

He kissed down my neck and buried his head between my breasts. "I missed these tits. You have no idea."

Wrapping my legs around his back, I moved my hips to match the rhythm of his hard thrusts. Before I knew it, I was coming so hard that I didn't know if I was having multiple orgasms in a row. It felt like several all running into each other.

Rush's body shook as he came inside of me. He pumped in and out slowly long after he'd finished. His eyes were still closed, as he seemed to be cherishing every last second of it.

He finally opened his eyes and kissed me softly on the forehead. "I don't care what doubts you're having...don't ever doubt that I love you, Gia."

After three rounds of sex, we were lying together in bed. Rush was rubbing gently over my stomach, and the baby started kicking. He placed his head on my belly and spoke to it. "I'm sorry for all that commotion. You can have your mommy back to yourself for a little while. But I might need her again soon."

Smiling like a fool, I could definitely get used to his conversations with the baby.

Rush cradled me in his arms. "I already told your dad that you're moving in with me."

I looked up at him in surprise. While it didn't shock me that he wanted me to move in with him, I wasn't sure if that was the greatest idea. Despite my doubts, I just couldn't say no. I didn't want to live apart from him, and moving into his place made the most sense.

Still, I couldn't help expressing my concerns. "I would love nothing more than to live in that beautiful house and to make a home for us there…although maybe it would be a good idea if I kept my apartment for a while, too…just in case."

Rush looked almost irate. "Fuck, Gia. I thought I told you to trust me. What do you mean…keep your apartment?"

"I do trust you…I just…feel like we've gone from zero to a hundred overnight. Might be smart for me to keep it for a while. It wouldn't be forever…just until after the baby is born."

He glared at me, the pain in his eyes palpable. "You think I'm gonna bail on you when the baby is born?"

There was simply no way to avoid admitting my concern to him. It was one thing to be okay with all of this when the baby was in my stomach. But once he or she was here and he looked into its eyes, how would he really feel? He believed he could love this baby…but how would he really *know*? What if it looked just like Elliott, and that caused Rush to snap? That was a worst-case scenario, of course, but I couldn't help wondering if that was even a remote possibility.

"I didn't say that I believed you would bail. I just…can't believe that you can say with one-hundred percent certainty that you know how you'll feel until the baby is actually here."

He looked so angry and frustrated with me for my lack of faith. "This is my fault," he finally said. "It's my fault that you're still doubting us. I led you to believe I couldn't handle any of this. And maybe it's not fair of me to expect you to feel confident overnight. I've done nothing to really prove anything to you, except give you my word. Time is what we need. So fine…keep the apartment if it makes you feel safer. I'll pay for it, and you can have it as a safety net. But you're not going to need it."

I straightened up against the headboard. "I'm not letting you pay."

"Gia…this isn't up for argument. You're keeping it because of me, because I made you believe you needed to. I'm paying for the damn apartment."

———

The next afternoon, Rush and I packed a bunch of my things into the Benz and drove them to his house.

I waited in his bedroom as he brought the boxes inside one by one. As I looked around at the massive space and the ocean just outside the French doors, there was only one word to describe how I was feeling: undeserving.

Rush walked over to his closet and started pushing his clothes to one side. "I obviously wasn't prepared for all of your stuff. But we'll figure it out. I can move my shit to the downstairs closet if this is not enough room for you."

"You shouldn't have to move anything anywhere. This is your house."

He stopped moving for a moment, then turned to me. "That's where you're wrong. As of today, it's *our* house."

He was now unpacking my ugly dolls one by one and placing them all in a row on the top shelf of his closet. Something about that touched me so much. To see my dolls taking permanent residence in Rush's closet was a very emotional experience.

Rush could see that I was starting to tear up and stopped what he was doing. "You know what? Let's forget about unpacking for a while. The sun's about to go down. Let's go chill outside and watch it." He reached his hand out to help me off the bed. "Come on."

Turns out, gazing at the sun setting over the ocean was just what the doctor ordered. My mood improved significantly with each minute that Rush and I sat out on his balcony and took in the salty air. The ocean was the best medicine, and I knew I'd be spending a lot of time out here in the coming weeks.

"I have an important question to ask you," he said suddenly.

My heart was pounding. *Please don't let it be a marriage proposal.* I could never accept that now. Not until the baby was born, and I knew things would be okay. I really didn't think that was what it was, but my heart and mind were racing nevertheless.

I cleared my throat. "What is it?"

"You know…this place is beautiful…but it's never really felt like home, because living alone never feels like home. It was just a house. And after I met you, it started to feel even emptier whenever I was here by myself. Because in contrast to how I feel when I'm with you, everything is empty. The only way this house could ever be a *home* is with you in it."

I squeezed his hand. "Thank you."

"Here's the thing. This house could burn down tomorrow, right? Anything can happen in life. We just don't know. I was up last night trying to figure out all of the ways I could convince you to trust in me, to believe that I don't have any intention of walking away. And I came to the conclusion that I was approaching it the wrong way."

"What do you mean?"

"To expect to be able to prove something a hundred percent is stupid. Even the smallest shred of doubt is still doubt. And it's normal to have doubts, because there is always uncertainty in life. We live every day knowing that there's a possibility we could die. Yet, we get up every day and do what we need to do anyway. Life shouldn't be about constantly trying to prove that we're safe from getting hurt. Life should be about living *with* uncertainty while we watch beautiful sunsets with the people we love."

Man, that was beautiful, and it made so much sense. I was waiting for something I would never really get: certainty. I'd probably always fear losing Rush. It was something I had to learn to live with.

"So, my question to you, Gia, is this: will you be uncertain with me?"

It was amazing what a difference a new perspective could make.

Be uncertain. Live anyway.

He was totally right. I'd been waiting for a safe feeling. It might never come. There would always be fear of losing him for one reason or another. And in focusing on the fear…I was losing the one thing that ever mattered…the only thing that ever really existed: *today.*

I let go and took a deep breath. "Yes. Yes, I will be uncertain with you."

In that moment, for the first time in a long time, I felt at peace. I gave up the fight to figure out tomorrow and chose to live for today.

———

Later that night, Rush was taking a shower when I decided to take a walk around the house. I stopped in the nursery and flicked the light on.

Everything was exactly the way it was when he'd first shown it to me. I ran my index finger along the mobile hanging over the crib. Despite everything we'd been through, Rush had never changed a thing in this room. That spoke volumes about his intentions all along.

I started to talk to my belly. "You're so lucky, you know that? You're gonna have the best daddy, who loves and protects you—just like I had. Except, unlike me…you'll have a mommy who loves you, too."

I felt the baby kick. "But, God, you'd better be a boy. Tony could handle a girl…but Rush? I don't know. I feel bad for any of the boys being born right about now if you turn out to be a girl."

His voice startled me. "You talking to my baby?"

His baby.

"Yes. We're talking about you."

"Nothing bad I hope, because when he takes one look at me, that's gonna be terrifying enough. I might scare the shit out of him. So, I need you to put in a good word in the meantime."

I laughed. "I was telling him how lucky he is to have you as a dad. He's gonna love you so much…just like I do."

Rush pulled me into a hug. He smelled so good, fresh out of the shower.

He let out the longest breath into my neck. "I want to tell Elliott this week. I hate to even bring it up…but the sooner we do it, the better. I want him to know where things stand, that in all of the ways that matter…I'm this baby's father. I just want to get the whole damn thing over with, so we can start moving on with our lives."

My stomach dipped. As much as it hurt me to think about, I knew it was inevitable and the right thing to do… to get it over with. "Okay. This week." I nodded. "We'll tell him this week."

CHAPTER 25

Gia

"Why don't we have you stand right behind her and wrap your arms around her stomach?"

"Gladly," Rush said as he enveloped me in his arms before nibbling at my neck.

Flash.

Flash.

Flash.

It was the afternoon of my prescheduled pregnancy photoshoot. Rush decided to accompany me to the City, so the photographer thought it would be a cool idea to have him in some of the photos with me. Personally, I had a feeling she was getting off on his being there, probably loved shooting *him* more than me. Overall, it was probably a bad idea... because with all of the touching, Rush was getting very excited.

Earlier, we had taken some shots of me alone wearing angel wings, an ode to Rush's love of winged women. Now Jenny was just focusing on capturing the two of us.

He continued to kiss the back of my neck while she snapped away.

She held up her large camera with the long lens. "That's it. Just like that. Kiss her neck again."

Flash.

Flash.

Flash.

I was laughing as he tickled my neck with his lips and could feel the swell of his erection behind me. Whoever thought it was a good idea to take photos of Rush kissing and fondling me while I was half-naked clearly didn't know my boyfriend was a horny preggophile.

"Why don't you come stand to the side of her?" she said.

Rush whispered into my ear, "Not sure I should move from behind you right now…I'm at full mast."

I broke out into laughter and told her, "Um…can you just continue taking photos with him behind me? We like this position."

Rush snorted.

The photographer scratched her chin and looked like she was pondering her next move. "How would you feel about taking your top all the way off and having Rush hold your breasts?"

Ummm.

I hesitated. "Uh…that wou—"

"I *love* that idea," he said.

She smiled at him and looked at me for approval. "Gia?"

I shrugged. "Sure…yeah."

Rush did the honors of slipping my shirt over my head. He unsnapped my bra and threw it on a nearby chair. Then he took his hands and cupped both of my breasts. His hands were barely able to fit around them anymore.

He let out a low moan, and I couldn't help but laugh at the fact that my maternity shoot had somehow turned into a porno.

———

Since we were already in the City, the plan was to pay a visit to Edward at the hospital before heading back home. Thankfully, he was stable and continuing to make small improvements.

Rush was in the hospital room with his father when I decided to head to the cafeteria to grab something to drink.

As I turned a corner, someone smacked right into me, causing me to lose my balance and fall onto the ground.

"Fancy meeting you here, Gia." His words cut like a knife. The smell of alcohol was immediately apparent on his breath, even from where I was lying on the floor.

Before I could find the words to respond to Elliott, Rush's voice registered from behind me.

"What the fuck is going on?"

Oh no.

"Rush, tell your girlfriend we need to stop meeting like this…with her down on her knees."

Rush was too upset about me being on the ground to even respond to that. He offered his hand and pulled me up. "Did he push you?"

"No, I fell. It was an accident."

He continued to ignore Elliott as he wrapped his hands around my face. "Are you okay?"

Elliott gave me a once over. "Were you always this curvy? What are you feeding her, Rush?"

He's such an asshole.

"She's pregnant, you fuckhead," Rush blurted out. "And you just knocked her to the ground."

Well, that was an interesting way to unleash that news. Rush looked at me slightly panicked that he'd said it, and I gave him a look that told him it was okay that he'd let it out.

Elliott squinted. "What do you mean, she's pregnant?"

Rush pulled me close. "I'm not sure how else to explain it."

"You're the father?"

Rush paused. "Yes."

Shit.

Elliott didn't even respond. He just looked between the two of us before storming past us and into Edward's room.

After he left, Rush looked at me. "I'm sorry for blurting it out. But I just couldn't tell him the truth right then and there."

Blowing out a shaky breath, I nodded. "No. I get it."

"It just didn't seem like the right time or place. Not that he's ever in a good frame of mind, but I'm not giving him news like that when he's piss-ass drunk. He may not even remember this." He rubbed my shoulder. "You sure you're okay?"

"Yeah…I'm fine."

For now.

"Let's get you home."

───────

Later that night, Rush and I were having a peaceful evening relaxing in front of the television with a tub of Chunky Monkey when his cell phone rang.

After he picked up, I could tell by his face that something was wrong.

He mouthed, "It's Elliott."

My heart sank.

Rush was quiet for a long time as he just listened. I could hear the muffled sound of Elliott's voice through the phone, although I wasn't able to hear what he was saying. Rush closed his eyes for several seconds then opened them.

"What is he saying?" I asked.

"Hold on a second," he simply said to his brother.

Rush placed his hand on my knee and whispered, "He's sobered up and put two and two together. He wants to know if I was lying about being the father."

My heart was racing. "Put him on speakerphone. I need to be the one to tell him."

"You don't have to do that."

"Yes, I do."

Rush did as I asked and said, "You're on speakerphone, Elliott. Gia is here."

"Elliott…" I said.

"Gia…" he said tauntingly.

I must have rehearsed how I was going to tell him a thousand times. In the end, my mind went blank, and I just said the first thing that came out.

"The night you and I were together resulted in my getting pregnant. I didn't know about my condition when I met and fell in love with your brother. Rush and I want to raise this baby together, and you don't need to be involved in its life, but you do need to know that it's yours."

Rush reached for my hand and squeezed it.

Elliott fell completely silent. All you could hear was his breathing for the longest time. Rush and I just kept looking at each other waiting for his response.

"How do I even know you're telling the truth?" he finally said.

"You were the only person I slept with before I found out. I obviously can't prove that to you, but it's the truth."

There was a long pause. "Did you know my wife is pregnant?"

"Yes," Rush said. "She told me."

"What you don't know is that Lauren is filing for divorce."

Shit.

Rush was biting his tongue. I knew he wanted to tell him that he deserved every bit of bad luck that came to him. But Rush was intentionally trying to be good for me. He didn't want to make things worse than they already were.

"You have a good woman, Elliott. You should try to figure out a way to make things work."

"Well, when she finds out I've impregnated your girlfriend, that's going to go off real well, don't you think? I'm sure she'll come running back."

"She doesn't need to know," Rush said.

"Lauren is not changing her mind about leaving me. She made that clear. So you see...I really have nothing to lose anymore."

"What the fuck does that mean?" Rush spewed.

"It means I'm gonna want a paternity test. My life is as fucked up as it gets right now. But you'd better believe if this baby is mine, I'm gonna make sure my rights are protected."

CHAPTER 26

Rush

"He's going to make me look like a whore. I got pregnant with a one-night stand, and now I'm dating his brother." Gia paced back and forth in front of the TV. "He's got a team of lawyers. What if he says that I'm unfit and goes for full custody? Could he take the baby? Oh my God. When I was in middle school, my dad made me go talk to the guidance counselor weekly. He was afraid that I was having a hard time because I got my period and didn't want to talk to him about it. I told her stuff that Elliott could use against me."

"Gia…"

"My dolls! We have to get rid of them immediately. What if they send a social worker to the house to make sure that I'm competent and they see that I burn dolls? They look like babies! They're going to think that I might toss my own child in a fire." She pulled at her hair and started to pace faster. "I'm writing a romance novel. What if they think I'm a degenerate who is obsessed with sex?"

"Gia…" I said louder. She still didn't hear me.

"Do you think Melody would lie for me? Say that I'm normal, and I'll be a good parent to my child? I think she'd make a good character witness."

"Gia…"

"I read in a gossip column that the Britney Spears-Kevin Federline custody battle cost over a million dollars. What if Elliott…"

I stood and took a step into her path, effectively stopping her in her tracks. "Gia."

Her body stood still, but her brain didn't.

"Oh my God! I should have bought the minivan. Why did you let me buy that fancy car? I'm going to look totally irresponsible. Do you think we can return it still? I only have a few hundred miles on it. Shit…I spilled a little orange juice on the rug the other day. Do you know anyone who cleans carpet?"

I took her cheeks into my hands and tilted her head up. "Gia."

She looked up, but *still* didn't hear me. "Maybe I shouldn't live here," she said. "That won't look good. Living out of wedlock is still frowned upon by a lot of people. Especially if they're older. I wonder if the judge will be old."

Giving up on getting her attention by calling her name, I did the one thing I knew would slow her down, even if just for a few moments. I pressed my lips to hers. She talked into my mouth for a few seconds before her brain caught up to her body. Then she wrapped her hands around my neck and gave me her tongue.

The kiss was only meant to refocus her, but fuck if my body didn't react immediately. I could've kept going. Hell, maybe I should've. We both had tension we needed to let go of. But I wanted her to hear what I had to say loud and clear—not through a post-orgasm haze. So I pulled back after a minute.

My girl was breathing heavy. It made me smile even in the middle of the nightmare that we'd just entered. "You good?" I whispered.

"Huh?"

I chuckled. "It's my turn to talk. Come sit down."

Gia sat on the couch, and I knelt down in front of her. I took both of her hands in mine.

"First off. Elliott might have money, but so do we."

"But…"

I pressed my lips to hers for another kiss. When she stopped trying to talk, I broke the connection again. "This conversation will go a lot faster if you could shut up, you know."

Her eyes widened. "Did you just tell me to shut up?"

I grinned. "I did. And I'll tell you to shut the fuck up again if you don't sit here and give me a chance to speak. For the record, you're welcome to tell me to shut the fuck up when I'm losing my mind and won't listen to you, too."

"I'm not losing my mind…I'm just worried. Elliott could…"

I leaned in and kissed her again, my lips moving against hers as I murmured, "Shut the fuck up, sweetheart."

When I pulled back yet again, she narrowed her eyes. "Fine. But I get to talk afterwards."

"Deal. Okay. So…as I was saying…Elliott might have money, but so do we. And before your brain gets stuck on how *we* don't have money but that *I* have money, I want to explain something to you. *One more time*. The reason that it took me so long to pull my head out of my ass and commit to you is that I couldn't make the decision to become a parent lightly. I am not in this to be Uncle Rush, Gia. I'm in this for the long haul. I'm in this to be Dad, just like you're in this to be Mom. That's what took me so long to wrap my brain around. I was scared. Because I needed to know that this was forever. And maybe you're not ready to hear this, but this is forever for me, Gia. I feel no fucking different than if you were my wife. I've committed. What's mine is yours and what's yours is mine. Maybe you're not understanding this because you haven't gotten there yourself yet. But I'm there. So, one last time...what's mine is yours. We have money. And if you try to separate what I have from what you have, I'm going to start to get upset and think that you're less committed to *me* than I am to *you*. So do me one favor?"

Gia had tears in her eyes. Her voice cracked. "What?"

"Shut the fuck up about money once and for all."

She laughed. "Okay."

"Moving on. Your middle school guidance counselor is not going to appear out of thin air and tell your twelve-year-old schoolgirl secrets. Just because you write romance novels doesn't make you a degenerate. Is Stephen King a psycho killer just because he writes twisted shit? No. So kick that crap from your mind, too. As far as the car—I'll trade in my Mustang tomorrow and drive a minivan if it makes you feel better. Although no one is going to be looking at the model of your car to determine if you're a good mother. And Melody would probably lie for you if you wanted her to, but she won't have to. She already thinks you're going to be an amazing mother. So don't worry about that either. The dolls..." I scratched my chin. "Okay. I'll give you that one.

It's a little wacky. But if Social Services ever does pop in, I promise to hide them for you. I'll eat them if I have to."

Gia smiled. "Are you done, crazy man?"

"Almost. Lastly, living out of wedlock. We can fix that in an hour if you're going to worry about that. While I'd prefer to surprise you with a nice ring someday because that's what you deserve, I'd go to the courthouse and marry the shit out of you tomorrow. You know why?"

Tears started to leak from her eyes. I wiped them away with my thumb.

"Why?" Her voice cracked.

"Because I love you, and I'm in this for good. A piece of paper isn't going to change that one way or the other."

Gia stared at me. Her eyes seemed to search deep into mine for something. Finding whatever she needed, her face turned serious. "You would really marry me, tomorrow, wouldn't you?"

"There isn't anything I wouldn't do for you, sweetheart."

———

Gia had fallen asleep a few hours ago. But I couldn't relax enough to let myself drift off. Even though I'd assured her that there was no way in hell that Elliott would get custody of the baby, I couldn't stop thinking about what it would be like if he even had visitation.

Edward had a long-term relationship with my mother before she'd gotten pregnant, and he had a good role model in his own father. Elliott had neither. He didn't know Gia at all, and he had watched the way his own father treated my mother and me. There was no doubt in my mind that Elliott would only see Gia's child as a pawn in a game to manipulate the two of us. It would be like my childhood all over again—seeking approval and love from a man who had no interest in me. I couldn't let that happen to Gia's child. To *our* child.

Old memories were haunting me as I lay in bed staring at my beautiful, sleeping girl. In sixth grade, my school held a father-son night. The kind where they tell you to wear deodorant, respect girls, and give you a clinical intro to the birds and the bees. My mother had thought it might be a good bonding experience, so she invited Edward to take me. I'd never have admitted it, but I was excited. My friends were all going with their dads. Joe Parma's dad had come straight from work and invited us to sit with them. He was a sanitation worker in the City and didn't have time to stop home and change. Edward wiped his hand off after he'd been forced to shake the man's hand. Then he spent the rest of the night making snide comments about how public school produced criminals. The next week, I smoked pot for the first time and stole a bicycle. Wouldn't have wanted to prove dear old dad wrong.

When I graduated high school, Edward mailed me a card. By then, I'd grown from being disappointed in my sperm donor to hating his fucking guts. I should've tossed the card in the garbage. Instead, I opened it to see if the prick had at least sent me a check. He had, but he'd also signed the card Edward, not Dad. I used the check and card as kindling to start a bonfire in the yard and accidentally set the shed on fire.

There was no way I wanted that constant disappointment for my child. Forced contact from a man who didn't give a shit about you was way worse than no communication. Look at Gia; she didn't even know her mother—yet she turned out more emotionally stable than most people with two parents. The continual reminder that you weren't wanted could really screw with a kid's head.

I needed to protect our son.

And I had a feeling I might be able to.

———————

The next morning, I woke up before Gia, even though I'd only slept for two hours. I drank three cups of coffee while writing out a list of things to do to set my plan into motion. At nearly nine, Gia padded into the kitchen wearing the shirt I'd worn yesterday. I fucking loved her waking up in my bed and wearing my clothes.

"Morning," she yawned and stretched her arms over her head. "What are you up to so early?"

"Early? It's almost nine o'clock, sleepyhead." I shifted in my seat and opened my arms. "Come here."

She plopped her fine ass down on my lap and leaned her head on my shoulder. "I hate not being able to drink coffee."

"I'll pick up some decaf on the way home tonight."

She pouted. "You have to work at the restaurant tonight?"

"Actually…I was hoping I could ask you to cover for me. I have some things I need to do today, and it's the winter bartender's first day. He worked for me last season, but I don't want to leave him alone on his first day back."

Gia perked up. "Me? You want me to be the manager?"

"Sure." I shrugged. "Why not?"

"Do I get to growl at people and bark orders like the regular manager?"

My lip twitched. "Absolutely. Give 'em hell."

She went to get up, but I gently yanked her back down onto my lap. "Wait a minute. Don't run away so soon. I need to talk to you about something else."

"Okay."

I took a minute to think about how I wanted to present things to her. In the end, I decided less was better. Once everything I planned was over, I'd give her all the details. But sharing too much information would definitely cause her anxiety to go into an uproar.

"After you fell asleep last night, I spent a lot of time going over the shit that went down with Elliott yesterday."

Her cheery face wilted. "Okay…"

"I want to ask you something. But I need you to trust me and not ask any questions. Just answer my question. Can you do that?"

"That's hard to say. How am I supposed to know if I can answer a question without knowing the question?"

"Let me ask you this…do you trust me?"

"You know I do."

"Do you trust that anything I do will be in our best interest?"

"Yes. Of course."

"Okay. So…if I could get rid of Elliott from our lives, is that what you'd want? What you'd *really* want for me, you and the baby?"

"Would you…"

I silenced her with two fingers pressed to her mouth and shook my head. "No questions. Remember? Just answer mine."

She closed her eyes for a few seconds and then took a deep breath.

"Well, since I'm not allowed to ask any questions, I'm going to preface my answer with a statement then. "You *cannot* kill Elliott." She paused. "But other than that, yes, that's absolutely what I'd want to happen."

I smiled and kissed her forehead. "Good enough. I gotta jump in the shower."

CHAPTER 27

Rush

"Are you sure you want to do this, son?"

Gerald Horvath, grandfather's old attorney, knew the long history between my father, brother, and me. I'd called him this morning to ask that he draw up an agreement for me. He'd agreed but also wanted to meet with me to discuss things.

"I'm positive."

He took off his glasses. "We're talking a lot of money here, Heathcliff."

"I don't care about the money."

Gerald smiled sadly. "I remember the day that I told you what your grandfather had left you. It troubled you more than anything."

"Money can buy a lot of things, but it's also the root of a lot of evils."

He nodded like he understood, slipped his glasses back on, and tossed two documents in front of me. "Well, I did what you asked. Although I had to word it a little differently so it could hold up in court if things ever came to that. But I think these two contracts give you the same effect that you're looking for."

Gerald gave me a little time to read through both documents, and then we talked about a few things he'd added himself that I hadn't thought about—a punitive damages clause, confidentiality clause, and some other legal mumbo jumbo that made sense when he explained them. When we were done, he sat back in his big leather chair and steepled his hands.

"You think he's going to take your offer?"

"He's pretty self-destructive lately. I'm not sure he'll be able to put what's best for him above his emotional immaturity."

"So how do you intend to convince him?"

I stood. "I don't. I need buy-in from the man on my next stop to help me do that."

"Jesus." I let myself into Elliott's apartment at seven that evening using the key I'd picked up from Lauren that morning. The place looked like a frat house at dawn after initiation night. Bottles of alcohol were strewn all over the floor, two naked women were passed out on the couches, takeout boxes littered the countertops, and shit was spilled everywhere. The only thing differentiating this scene from a college banger was that the tightly rolled up bills sitting on a mirror on the living room table were hundreds and not ones, and the view outside the window was of the Manhattan skyline instead of drunken teens passed out on a muddy lawn.

I walked over to one of the women and used my foot to shake her awake. "Time to get up, sweetheart."

She turned and opened one squinty eye, using her hand to shade it from the light. "The other guy only paid for one."

Great. I scooped up a pile of clothes from the floor and tossed them at her. "Party's over. Get dressed."

Then I nudged the other sleeping beauty. "Time to take your friend and go home."

While the two of them groaned and tried to figure out whose clothes belonged to whom, I went in search of Elliott. Unfortunately for me, I found him naked and sprawled out across his bed. At least he was face down. I checked he was still breathing and decided to put on a pot of coffee before waking that one up.

One of the two ladies walked into the kitchen. She held onto the doorway as she spoke. "Do we get a tip?"

Elliott's wallet happened to be on the counter next to me. I opened it and pulled out the thick wad of cash. Handing it to the woman, I smiled. "Take it all. My treat."

She fanned the bills, saw a few hundreds, and stuffed it into her bra. "Thanks, cutie. You sure you don't want a little parting gift goodbye? I bet you're way more fun than your friend."

"No, thanks. I'm good."

After I locked the door behind them, I grabbed a garbage bag, tossed in every bottle of alcohol in the house, and dumped it in the garbage chute. Then I headed back to my loving brother and gave him a little kick, too.

"Rise and shine, big bro."

He snored louder in response.

A few more attempts still didn't wake the fucker. So I headed back to the living room, sprayed some Lysol on a chair, and made myself comfortable. I hadn't slept too well, anyway, last night, and I needed Elliott sober. It looked like I'd be waiting it out.

Around six-thirty in the morning, the idiot finally stirred. I'd drawn the blinds last night, so the living room was still dark. My eyes were shut when Elliott walked out from the bedroom, and he brushed against the chair I sat in.

"I hope that was your fucking arm."

"What the…"

"Relax, it's your baby brother. Not the pimp coming to collect his two whores." I stood.

"What the fuck are you doing here?" Elliott flipped on a light.

"Someone had to show your guests out. You're shit for a host."

"Fuck you." He walked to the kitchen and poured a glass of water from the tap.

I shook my head at his bikini underwear. "Nice banana hammock. Don't your balls get uncomfortable in those things? My nuts need room to hang. Then again, maybe you got peanuts instead of man balls."

He chugged two full glasses of water before turning around again. "What the fuck do you want?"

"I'm glad you asked. I want Gia's child to be mine and to be rid of you and the entire Vanderhaus family once and for all."

Elliott snickered. "We can't always get what we want. Can we?"

I started to lose patience. If I was going to get anywhere with making this happen, it was probably best if my fist didn't connect with his face and we steered clear of the jabs.

"Get dressed. We need to go see Edward."

A glimmer of vulnerability peeked through. "Why? Is he okay?"

"He's fine. I just went to visit him last night. Unlike you."

"I'll go see him later then."

"No. *We'll* go now. Together. The three of us have urgent business to discuss, and I've been waiting for your wasted ass all night." My tone told him I wasn't fucking around.

"Fine. But I'm only going because I don't have the energy to throw you the fuck out."

Yeah, sure. That's the reason.

Neither of us said a word on the way to Mount Sinai. Edward was sitting up in bed reading a newspaper when we walked into his private room. He folded it and spoke to Elliott. "You look terrible. Cut the crap, get over the shit with your wife, and get back to work. Women are a dime a dozen. You'll find a new one to keep the house and look good on your arm. But the company needs you right now."

I shook my head. *Great fatherly advice.*

Edward looked to me. "Why don't we get down to business?"

Pulling two contracts from the envelope, I handed them to Elliott. "I'll sign over everything Grandfather left to me, except for the house I live in and the restaurant. You can have all my shares in Vanderhaus Holdings, the three Hampton rentals, and all the stocks he left me."

"And what do you want in return?"

"I want you to give up your parental rights to Gia's baby and agree not to come within a hundred feet of either me or her again. Apparently, it's unconscionable to make one contract where I pay you to give up your rights, so Gerald made two separate contracts. One where you give up your parental rights out of the goodness of your heart. And the other a contractual agreement where I pay you a small fortune to not come within ten feet of me and Gia."

"Why the hell would I sign that?"

"Because the two of you will have more money than you'll ever need, and you won't need to get my buy-in on anything ever again."

Elliott smirked at me. "I don't need your money. And having this little bastard to lord over you will bring me years of enjoyment torturing the two of you."

I spoke through gritted teeth. "Say one more derogatory comment about Gia or the baby, and you'll be spending a month in the bed next to your father. I'm not screwing around, Elliott."

Edward sighed. "Alright, alright. This is a business transaction. We don't need to be barbaric about it."

I kept my eyes glaring at Elliott but spoke to Edward. "Tell your son what it's like to have a child you don't want, *Dad*."

Edward didn't miss a beat, and didn't even attempt to soften the edge of his words. "Impregnating your brother's mother was the biggest regret of my life. To have a child you never wanted constantly looking to you for something you just don't feel is a bothersome burden you don't need."

I felt the usual stab in the heart, but for once it didn't matter. The only thing that mattered was Gia and the baby.

Edward looked at me and then back to Elliott. "Sign the papers, Elliott. Don't let a second generation taint our family name. We'll never have to deal with the two of them again and our company will be fully back in the hands of its rightful owners."

In order to truly move on, you have to stop looking back. I hadn't even realized that was what I'd been doing until now. But it was. Elliott signed the papers and extended them in his hand to me. It felt like a weight I'd been carrying around had suddenly been lifted from my shoulders. Who knew giving away a small fortune, saying goodbye to your father and brother for the very last time, and taking on the responsibility of a baby on the way could be so cathartic.

I took one last look at Edward and Elliott, then nodded and took the signed papers. "Have a good life."

CHAPTER 28

Rush

The weeks that followed Elliott's signing his rights away were some of the most peaceful Gia and I had ever experienced together.

Let's face it, we hadn't had too many moments without drama in the entire course of our relationship. We'd earned this, and dammit, I was enjoying every second of it. Waking up to her every morning and sleeping next to her every night was bliss.

We'd spend our mornings out on the balcony overlooking the ocean and spend our evenings the exact same way. Every day I'd notice her belly growing more and count my blessings that the little baby inside was truly mine in every way that mattered. I couldn't believe how easy it had been to buy Elliott off. I wondered if he'd come to regret his decision someday, but that was his problem, not mine.

Another positive of this new life? I didn't miss the business side of things at all. I still had The Heights and a damn nice roof over my head for my family, and that was all I needed. No more showing up to bullshit board meetings in the City and no more having to fight with Edward and Elliott.

I'd basically paid for my freedom back in more ways than one.

Gia and I were pretty well prepared for the baby's arrival. The nursery was finished and stocked, and we'd taken Lamaze classes. We were as ready as we were going to be. Now with only a couple of weeks to go until her due date, I felt like there was really only one thing I wanted to accomplish before the birth—I wanted to put a ring on my woman's finger. And there was no way I could do that without thinking up something fucking spectacular.

This idea came to me one night. Since Gia managed to turn her book in on time to her editor, the manuscript was out of her hands. Still, I wondered if I could somehow snag an advance copy before she even saw it in print. My plan was to surprise her with it and stick the ring inside the pages. She wouldn't see it coming because she'd initially think the surprise was the book itself. Then, boom…the ring would be inside. I hadn't worked out all the details yet, but I also planned to take her to her favorite restaurant close to home. I would've loved to take her away, but we couldn't travel too far anymore.

Her agent had come through for me. She spoke to the publisher and had them send an early paperback of Gia's novel. I felt almost guilty for seeing it before she did, but I knew she was going to freak when she realized why I had it. Apparently, it wasn't the final version because the book was still in editing, but they were able to print me a copy of it anyway. I'd told the agent to ship it to The Heights so that Gia didn't see it.

I was now sitting in my car outside of the jeweler's building. Taking the book out of the padded envelope, I rubbed my hand over the glossy cover that featured a woman sitting on a beach looking introspective. Gia had wanted a sexier cover, but the publisher nixed that idea, saying that Gia's vision was too racy for bookstore shelves. I was so damn proud of her for getting to this point. She'd written this novel during the toughest time of her life. She'd pushed through, gotten it done, and met her deadline. My girl wrote a freaking book. She was a badass.

After I opened it, I froze when I looked at the first chapter heading.

Chapter One: Rush

She'd named him Rush? Get outta here. No fucking way.

She always joked about doing that, but I never actually thought she'd go through with it. Back when we had that bet about whether I could quit smoking and she could quit candy, she'd said she would name her character Rush if she lost. Of course, I was the one who lost, so I ended up fixing her car instead, the car that I'd already fixed before she even realized it. I never imagined she'd actually name her character after me.

Damn.

I was supposed to be surprising her, but it seemed I was the one shocked. I felt bad for ruining what was probably supposed to be a surprise for *me*. Well, I didn't really feel that bad—because this was going to be a bomb-ass proposal.

I put the book back in the envelope and ventured into the jewelry store to pick up the engagement ring I'd selected a couple of weeks earlier.

The owner, who was dressed in an elegant, crisp suit, approached me as soon as I entered. "Hello, Mr. Rushmore. We have the ring sized and cleaned for you."

"Great. Thank you." I sat down and leaned over the counter that displayed dozens of diamond rings through the glass. "Let's see it."

The jeweler opened the small, black velvet box to show me the two and a half carat round diamond with a pavé diamond band.

I shook my head slowly and let out a deep breath as I held up the ring between my thumb and index finger. "Beautiful. I hope she likes it."

Now I just needed to figure out when I was going to execute my plan.

"If no further adjustments are needed, we can process payment, and you can take the ring home today," he said.

"Yeah. Let's do it. Thank you."

I wiped my forehead. Jesus, was I sweating?

It wasn't that I was nervous to get engaged, just the opposite. I wanted everything to be perfect and hoped Gia wanted to get married as much as I did.

The man asked me if I needed a bag, but I told him no, slipping the ring box inside my jacket where I felt it would be safer. I didn't want to run the risk that Gia would find the bag anyway.

When I returned to my car, I realized I'd left my phone on the passenger seat while I was inside the jewelry store. It was lit up with missed calls, texts, and voicemail notifications. All were from Gia.

Gia: I don't know where you are. I've been trying to call you but you're not answering, I'm pretty sure my water just broke. I tried to call my doctor but couldn't get him, so

I'm just taking myself to the hospital. I'm scared. My due date isn't for another two weeks!! I can't be having this baby now!

Shit!

My heart was frantic as I typed, my hands shaking.

Rush: Where are you now? Are you there yet?

I waited a full minute, and there was no response. Then I pressed play on the most recent voicemail as I started the car and sped away.

"Hey, Rush. I texted already, figured I would try calling again. I don't know where you are, but I really wish you'd pick up. They just admitted me. They checked me and told me I'm about to have this baby. I may not get to call you again. If you get this, please hurry."

It felt like my head was spinning. The time on the message was ten minutes ago. As I headed in the direction of the main road that would take me to the hospital, I came upon standstill traffic.

Banging my hands against the steering wheel, I screamed, "Fuck!" I beeped the horn. "Come on!"

Traffic wasn't moving. In the distance, I could see a bunch of walkers with numbers plastered onto their chests. They were doing a 5K or some shit. That must have been what was holding things up.

I couldn't afford to wait. When I spotted a guy standing on the sidewalk with his bike, I jumped out of the car and raced over to him.

Opening my wallet, I took out every last bill. It had to have been at least five hundred bucks.

"My girlfriend is in labor. Traffic isn't moving. I need your bike. I'll give you all my money and my car for the afternoon."

He took one look at my Mustang, which was idling with the door open and said, "Sweet."

I knew it was a risk, but it didn't matter to me what happened to the damn car. All that mattered was that Gia and the baby were going to be okay and that I could be there.

We quickly exchanged numbers before I hopped on his bike and started flying down the road, weaving in and out of cars and people. The bike was squeaking; it was old as shit. I hadn't been on an actual bicycle in years. What they said about not forgetting how to ride one was apparently true.

It felt like all the air had been sucked out of my body by the time I arrived at South Hampton Hospital. Sweat was pouring off me. It was a good thing we were in a hospital because there was a decent chance I might collapse.

I ran to the front desk. "Where is Labor and Delivery?"

"Fourth floor."

Out of breath, I ran to the elevators and banged several times on the up button.

When I got upstairs, I went straight to the nurses' station. "My girlfriend, Gia Mirabelli, is in labor. Help me find her."

"Are you the father of the baby?"

"Yes."

"Your name?"

"Ru…" I stopped myself. "Heathcliff Rushmore."

"ID, please?"

I took my license out of my wallet and handed it to her.

"Excuse me a moment." The woman got up and walked down the hall.

Did she just fucking walk off and leave me?

Where the hell is Gia?

She returned with a plastic bracelet that she wrapped around my wrist. Then looked up at me and smiled. "Come right this way."

My pulse was racing as I followed her down the hall. I looked down at the bracelet, which simply said *Mirabelli* along with a bunch of numbers.

When she opened the door to Gia's room, I nearly fell over. Whereas I'd previously been in a rush, everything came to a screeching halt.

Time just slowed down.

My heart squeezed with an unidentifiable feeling as I walked toward the bed where Gia was lying with a beautiful baby clutched to her chest, its fingers and toes moving around.

It was alive.

My baby.

My eyes filled with tears as I bent my head down to kiss its soft head that had a full mane of dark hair.

Still staring at the baby in awe, I whispered, "I'm so sorry I wasn't here, Gia. I did everything I could to get here once I got your message. I'd gone into a store without my phone, and there was traffic and—"

"It's okay. You probably couldn't have made it anyway. It happened so fast. Ten minutes after I got here, she came out. Everything turned out okay. She's here."

I swallowed. "She?"

She smiled, and her voice was hoarse. "Yes, we have a daughter."

That took a few seconds to sink in.

"A daughter?"

"Yes." Gia was beaming.

Caressing her little face with my thumb, I watched in awe as Gia tried to get the baby to latch onto her breast. "How could I have been so wrong?" I laughed as I lowered myself down to kiss her head again, taking in her scent. She smelled so sweet—she smelled like Gia. I loved her so much already that my heart was literally hurting from the feeling.

As we sat there in silence, fear started to fill me. This was gonna be a long eighteen years. Let's face it…more than that—a lifetime. All of the visions of doing manly things with my son went out the window. What did I know about having a girl? Nothing. All I knew was that I already loved her more than life itself. That would have to be enough until I could figure this out.

A doctor suddenly walked in. "Hello! Congratulations. Just checking in." He turned to me. "I'm Dr. Barnes. You are?"

I looked him dead in the eyes and answered, "Fucked. I have a daughter. I'm *fucked*."

CHAPTER 29

Gia

It had only been one day, but it already felt like we'd had her forever, like I couldn't imagine a time without her.

We still hadn't named our little girl. We had a ton of boy names picked out but nothing for a girl, so we needed to really think on it.

Rush had just come in with lunch from the Mexican place down the street. The baby was sleeping next to me in the little hospital crib after her last feeding. My dad had just left. It was the perfect window to grab a bite to eat before someone came in to check my vitals or the baby woke up to nurse.

Just as I'd unwrapped my burrito, an unexpected visitor appeared in the doorway.

Rush's mouth was full when he wiped his hands. He looked shocked when he said, "Edward…"

He nodded. "Heathcliff."

Edward was overdressed, wearing a long, wool overcoat.

Rush stood up and moved in front of the crib. It seemed like he was instinctively protecting our daughter. "What are you doing here?"

"Lauren told me where to find you. I came to see my granddaughter…and to talk to you."

It was surprising to see Edward here, not only because of his relationship with Rush, but because of his health. He must have had a driver waiting right outside to take him immediately back home.

Edward looked down at the sleeping baby. "She's beautiful like her mother."

I swallowed, not knowing how to respond. "Thank you."

He looked at Rush. "Can we go somewhere and talk?"

"No. Anything you have to say, you can say in front of Gia."

"Okay." Edward slowly sat down. "Something has been weighing on me for months."

Rush took a seat and sucked in his jaw. "Alright…"

"When you came to my hospital room with Elliott, to propose your agreement, I said some things that I need to explain, namely that getting your mother pregnant was the biggest regret of my life, that you were a burden."

"Yeah…I definitely heard it all the first time. You don't need to rehash."

My heart was breaking for Rush. That bastard. I never knew he'd said all that. Why did he even come here?

Edward looked like he was struggling with his words. "I need you to know that I didn't mean a word of it. I knew what was needed to get Elliott to sign to your agreement. He needed my approval, as he does with every decision he makes. I knew if I didn't choose my words wisely, that he might never give you the freedom you needed. So I lied and said those things to convince him to give you what you wanted, to sway things in your favor. It was the least I could do for you."

Rush stayed silent while Edward went on.

"I heard a lot of the things you said to me when I was in the hospital. I couldn't open my eyes or speak, but that didn't mean everything you said and did went unnoticed. Although I don't understand why you felt the need to be there when my behavior toward you over the years has been less than admirable, I want you to know how thankful I am for that and how proud I am of the man that you've become, even though I never say it." Edward let out a shaky breath. "You are *not* my biggest regret. My biggest regret is that I never knew how to be a father to you. That's something I can't ever change and something I will regret until the end of my days."

There was a long moment of silence.

Rush, who hadn't been looking at Edward, finally turned to him. "Okay. Is that all you came to say?"

"No." He stood up slowly. "I've created a trust for your daughter. It will contain a significant inheritance when she turns eighteen."

"I don't want your money."

"You don't have a choice in the matter. It will be in her name regardless of how you feel. She can make the decision at that time as to what she wants to do with the money. I just wanted to let you know that I've set it up. I'll have my attorney forward all of the details." Edward walked over to the crib. He reached his hand inside and brushed a finger along his granddaughter's cheek before turning his attention toward me. "Congratulations."

"Thank you," I said. My ability to talk seemed to be limited to those two words since he'd arrived.

And then Edward simply walked out.

Rush, who'd been stoic throughout his visit, closed his eyes briefly and let out a breath. Then I saw a single teardrop fall from his eyes. As much as Rush tried to have people believe that he didn't need his father's love, that was far from the truth. And even though I suspected things would never be great between Edward and Rush, I was happy that our daughter's birth could help Edward admit to some of his mistakes and do what he could to atone for them.

Rush turned to me as he wiped his eyes. "You didn't just see that, okay?"

I smiled and whispered, "Okay."

A nurse walked in with some paperwork. "So, not to pressure you, but here is the birth certificate form. It would be best if you could select a name for your daughter before you leave the hospital, so we can help you process everything. I'll leave it here with you."

Rush looked at me as he held our nameless kid. "Damn... we'd better decide, huh?"

We were no closer to a name than we were yesterday, having vetoed all of each other's suggestions.

Rush looked down at the baby in his arms. "You know what the problem is? There's no name good enough for my beautiful angel. Nothing is good enough."

Then it hit me.

That was it!

The angel hanging in his car.

The winged women he drew who looked like they were part-angel, part-fairy.

"Why not Angel, then?" I asked.

He scratched his chin. "Hmm. I never even thought of that." Rush looked at her for several seconds then smiled. "I think I freaking love that, actually." He bent down to kiss her head. "My angel's name is…Angel. It's perfect."

———————

That night, Rush must have thought I was asleep in my hospital bed when he began talking in a low voice to our daughter.

I was turned away from him and had been napping, so he couldn't see that I was awake.

"I'm gonna screw up a lot, Angel. I just know it. I need you to bear with me, okay? I promise to try my best. I'm never gonna let you down intentionally, but it will happen unintentionally sometimes. I can guarantee you that."

I couldn't help smiling to myself as I listened to his one-sided conversation.

"Like…I'll give you a prime example. I don't know if you realize this…but I screwed up in a big way right out of the gate. I missed your birth. What father does that? You probably didn't even know. You might have been a little too busy, you know, coming into the world and all to notice, but yeah. I wasn't here. And I will always kick myself for that because I can never get that moment back. Ever."

I could hear him kiss her.

"Someday I'll tell you why I was late." He paused. "Okay…you convinced me. I'll tell you now. You know… your Mommy and I…we haven't had an easy road to get to where we are now. There were lots of moments when I didn't think we would make it. And almost from the very beginning, it was a crazy ride. Your mother has a dirty mouth, you know. It was one of the first things that attracted me. But

I love that about her. I love *everything* about her—and about you. Anyway, I digress…got sidetracked thinking about your mom. I was telling you why I missed out on you being born. I wanted to plan something really special. I was out buying your Mommy a pretty diamond ring because I wanted to ask her to marry me before you got here. But I missed my chance because you came early. I had this elaborate plan of how I was gonna ask her. Did you know your Mommy wrote a book? I planned to surprise her with the first copy of it all nice and printed and then stick the ring inside as a double surprise. But I'm not sure that's even good enough anymore…because look at what she did…she gave me *you*. I feel like I have to come up with the most amazing proposal ever now…something even bigger…even more spectacular than what I had in mind. What do you think? You think I can pull off the best proposal ever?"

I smiled and closed my eyes.

I think you just did, Rush.

EPILOGUE

Rush

"Come on, just humor me," I said.

Gia shook her head. "There is no way I'm gonna fit into that thing."

"It's not gonna fit you the same, but that's why I want to see it…with all these curves." I held my hands together in begging position. "Please? It's my birthday."

"Your birthday is next week."

I raised my brows. "Early birthday gift?"

My mission today was to get Gia to try on her old yellow bikini. I had such fond memories of that thing, particularly the time she taunted me in it back before we were together. The problem was…she was eight-months pregnant now and didn't think she could fit into it. *Details.*

I kept flashing her my puppy dog eyes until she finally gave in.

Gia sighed. "Alright."

I fist pumped and not so patiently waited on the bed while she took it out of the drawer and slipped it on. With a view of her back, I gawked at the tattooed wings I'd managed to permanently ink onto her lower back right after Angel's birth, before she got pregnant again.

Yeah, I sort of knocked Gia up again two months after Angel was born.

It wasn't even intentional, I swear. It was an accident, but one I didn't regret because it gave me nine more months of enjoying her gorgeous, pregnant body, this time with the added pleasure of knowing that I was the one who made her that way. It doesn't get any hotter than that for an incorrigible preggophile.

We were under the impression that it was harder to get pregnant while breastfeeding. Whoops! And even though it would have been ideal to have more space between kids, in some ways, it was kind of nice to be having them close together. Then we could take a nice long break from having more, if she even wanted that. I knew I did, but it was her body, and that would be her decision. I knew she wouldn't be getting pregnant for a long while after this, though.

In one month, she was going to be giving birth to our son, Patrick. I was stoked. And that meant Patrick and Angel would be what are considered "Irish twins," babies born less than a year apart.

She twirled around to model the bikini, the pieces of yellow material barely covering her parts. "This thing used to belong to Riley, but I never gave it back because I loved it so much. Well, that was back when I could fit into it." Gia stuck her ass out. "What do you think?"

I gestured down to my bulging crouch. "What does it look like I think?"

She bit her lip as she gazed at my package. "Do you realize that in the entire time you've known me, I've only *not* been pregnant for two months?"

"Damn. That's kind of crazy when you put it that way." I pulled her on top of me. "Come here."

As pregnant as she was, Gia was helping support us. She'd gotten another book contract, and she would write during the day while helping me manage The Heights on the nights when Tony could watch Angel. Gia's dad had taken an early retirement from the police force and moved out to the Hamptons to be closer to us. He got a part-time gig working security at the beach and was renting a small apartment not far from The Heights.

Gia and I still hadn't gotten married. I kinda liked the idea of living in sin while she was knocked up. Even though she wore my ring on her finger, we agreed to do the whole wedding thing the right way with all the bells and whistles after our son was born.

Our son.

I loved the sound of that. See…I wasn't that off base in feeling like I was having a boy. I felt that boy coming in my bones. He was just a little late, that's all.

My sweet Angel baby was napping while Gia and I enjoyed this alone time. Thankfully, Elliott never violated any of the terms of the agreement we made when it came to our daughter. Lauren took him back, gave birth to their own baby girl, and as far as I knew, Lauren still didn't know the truth about Angel.

I reached over to the bureau and grabbed the sunscreen, squeezing a large dollop into my hand.

Gia's eyes widened. "What are you doing?"

"Lie on your back. I'm reminiscing about the first time I ever saw you in this bikini. Remember when you taunted me, asking me to rub this shit all over you when I was trying to resist you?"

She snickered. "Yes. That was fun."

"I bet it was. I jerked off for three days straight after."

"Except now there's no way I could lie on my stomach, so you'll have to take care of me from the front instead." She teased. "Could you go a little lower?"

Just like the first time, my breathing was erratic, and my dick immediately stiffened as I rubbed my hands into her skin.

"Lower," she said.

This was giving me major déjà vu.

She closed her eyes and was making the sexiest sounds as I began to remove her bikini bottom.

Just as things were starting to get good, Gia's cell rang.

"Don't get it," I snapped.

She lifted her head to glance over at the phone. "It's my dad. I should pick up."

I groaned and rolled over onto my back.

"Hey, Dad." After a while, she glanced over at me, looking almost concerned. "Uh…I guess."

Blinking my eyes, I leaned up against the headboard and continued listening to what she was saying.

"How do you even know she's interested?" Gia smiled at me and rolled her eyes. At least I knew it wasn't anything serious.

"Alright. I'll text it to you." She paused. "Okay. Bye, Daddy." She hung up and let out a breath of frustration.

I placed my hand on her stomach. "What was that all about?"

"It seems my father wants your mother's number. He thinks it would be a good idea to call Melody and invite her out for—in his words—dinner and dancing."

I snickered. "Uh-oh."

My mom had broken up with her boyfriend about six months ago, so she was available. I always kind of suspected Tony liked her. During Angel's christening, my mother and Gia's father sat together the whole time and seemed to be really getting along.

Gia shook her head. "I don't know about this."

As weird as it might have been to imagine them together, I couldn't think of a better guy I'd want dating my mother than Tony.

Shrugging my shoulders, I said, "I don't know…I think it'd be kind of cool."

"Isn't our family dynamic unconventional enough already? I'd prefer it if I wasn't inadvertently marrying my stepbrother!"

I bent my head back in laughter. "Didn't you read a book like that once?"

"Yes! But it was fiction! *Fiction,* Rush."

This was amusing me to no end. "Not sure you're gonna have a choice in the matter."

Gia cringed. "Don't say that!"

"Come here, Sissy," I teased, pulling her close to me on the bed.

She caressed my face and said, "Fortunately, Gia fell in love with Rush long before she found out about this potentially unsettling development."

I kissed her nose. "Unfortunately, even if she hadn't, Rush would have pursued her hard anyway until she finally gave in."

"Fortunately, with the right coercion, Gia could probably learn to make this taboo fantasy really work for her."

Fuck yes.

My excitement was halted when, right on cue, Angel's cries resonated from the nursery monitor that was sitting on the nightstand.

I laid my head in frustration on Gia's belly. "Unfortunately, Rush won't be getting laid this afternoon, will he?"

She laughed and patted my back before getting up.

When she came back and planted my baby girl on my chest, something I'd once said to Gia came to mind, and the truth of it was clearer than ever in that moment.

There really *was* no more *unfortunately* in our story.

Dear Readers,

We hope you've enjoyed reading Rush and Gia's story in *Rebel Heir and Rebel Heart.* We love to stay in touch with our readers and invite you to join our mailing list and receive back these **FREE** fun short stories!

Dry Spell is a short story—a fun, twenty-minute beach, bath or bed time read.

Jaded and Tyed is a novelette—meant to be read in an hour or two. It's perfect for anytime!

Both are exclusively yours for signing up for our mailing list today!

Visit https://www.subscribepage.com/2FreeBooks and you'll receive back these exclusive stories.

FREE NOW

ACKNOWLEDGEMENTS

We would like to thank the amazing bloggers who support our books and help spread the excitement for each new release. Without you, many readers may not have found us, and we are eternally grateful for all of the time and dedication that you give to us.

To Julie – Through the good, the bad, and the ugly, you're right there with us. Thank you for your cherished friendship. *Moore* to come!

To Elaine – Thank you for letting us drive you nuts with our short turnarounds and crazy schedule.

To Eda – Thank you for your excellent proofreading skills and for giving this project the final eyes it needed.

To Luna – We hated to share you with the world, but your talent couldn't be contained. We are so excited to watch your new business grow and flourish! www.heartandsolgraphics.com

To Erika – Thank you for all of your support for this duet, including being our final gatekeeper.

To Sommer – We couldn't have asked for better covers for this duet! Thank you for bringing Rush's story alive in your design.

To Dani – Thank you for organizing this release and for all of your support.

To our (super) agent, Kimberly Brower – Ari Gold's got nothing on you! Thank you for being such a badass for us.

Last but not least, to our readers – We are so lucky to have the best readers in the world! Thank you for your excitement, support and encouragement. You make our dreams possible!

Much love,
Penelope and Vi

OTHER BOOKS BY PENELOPE WARD & VI KEELAND

Rebel Heir

Dear Bridget, I Want You

Mister Moneybags

Playboy Pilot

Stuck-Up Suit

Cocky Bastard

OTHER BOOKS BY
PENELOPE WARD

Gentleman Nine

Drunk Dial

Mack Daddy

RoomHate

Stepbrother Dearest

Neighbor Dearest

Sins of Sevin

Jake Undone (Jake #1)

Jake Understood (Jake #2)

My Skylar

Gemini

OTHER BOOKS BY VI KEELAND

Standalone novels
Sex, Not Love
Beautiful Mistake
EgoManiac
Bossman
The Baller
First Thing I See

Life on Stage series (2 standalone books)
Beat
Throb

MMA Fighter series (3 standalone books)
Worth the Fight
Worth the Chance
Worth Forgiving

The Cole Series (2 book serial)
Belong to You
Made for You

YA/NA Novel
Left Behind

CPSIA information can be obtained
at www.ICGtesting.com
Printed in the USA
LVHW041241080520
655241LV00001B/97